MEN AT WORK

- ◆ Janelle Denison
- ◆ Nina Bangs
- ◆ MaryJanice Davidson

ᛒ

BERKLEY SENSATION, NEW YORK

THE BERKLEY PUBLISHING GROUP
Published by the Penguin Group
Penguin Group (USA) Inc.
375 Hudson Street, New York, New York 10014, USA
Penguin Group (Canada), 90 Eglinton Avenue East, Suite 700, Toronto, Ontario M4P 2Y3, Canada
(a division of Pearson Penguin Canada Inc.)
Penguin Books Ltd., 80 Strand, London WC2R 0RL, England
Penguin Group Ireland, 25 St. Stephen's Green, Dublin 2, Ireland (a division of Penguin Books Ltd.)
Penguin Group (Australia), 250 Camberwell Road, Camberwell, Victoria 3124, Australia
(a division of Pearson Australia Group Pty. Ltd.)
Penguin Books India Pvt. Ltd., 11 Community Centre, Panchsheel Park, New Delhi—110 017, India
Penguin Group (NZ), Cnr. Airborne and Rosedale Roads, Albany, Auckland 1310, New Zealand
(a division of Pearson New Zealand Ltd.)
Penguin Books (South Africa) (Pty.) Ltd., 24 Sturdee Avenue, Rosebank, Johannesburg 2196,
South Africa

Penguin Books Ltd., Registered Offices: 80 Strand, London WC2R 0RL, England

This is a work of fiction. Names, characters, places, and incidents either are the product of the
authors' imaginations or are used fictitiously, and any resemblance to actual persons, living or dead,
business establishments, events, or locales is entirely coincidental. The publisher does not have any
control over and does not assume any responsibility for author or third-party websites or their
content.

MEN AT WORK

A Berkley Sensation Book / published by arrangement with the authors

PRINTING HISTORY
Berkley Sensation trade paperback edition / December 2004
Berkley Sensation mass market edition / November 2005

Copyright © 2004 by The Berkley Publishing Group.
"Slow Hands" by Janelle Denison copyright © 2004 by Janelle Denison.
"Color Me Wicked" by Nina Bangs copyright © 2004 by Nina Bangs.
"The Fixer-Upper" by MaryJanice Davidson copyright © 2004 by MaryJanice Davidson Alongi.
Excerpt from *Born to Be Wilde* by Janelle Denison copyright © 2005 by Janelle Denison.
Cover art by Franco Accornero. Cover design by Rita Frangie.
Interior text design by Kristin del Rosario.

ISBN: 0-425-20683-1

BERKLEY® SENSATION
Berkley Sensation Books are published by The Berkley Publishing Group,
a division of Penguin Group (USA) Inc.,
375 Hudson Street, New York, New York 10014.
BERKLEY SENSATION and the "B" design are trademarks belonging to Penguin Group (USA) Inc.

PRINTED IN THE UNITED STATES OF AMERICA

10 9 8 7 6 5 4 3 2 1

Contents

SLOW HANDS

Janelle Denison

CHAPTER ◆ ONE

Tess Monroe gazed at the breathtakingly gorgeous man standing a few feet away from her and had to admit that Morgan Kane only grew finer with age. Every time she'd seen him over the past eight years he seemed sexier and more virile than before. And today was no exception.

With his back to her and unaware of her presence as he used an electric sander to smooth out the piece of wood on his work bench, she took a moment to appreciate what made him so stunningly male—most precisely the lean, toned physique guaranteed to turn feminine heads and illicit women's deepest, most erotic fantasies.

He'd certainly been the object of her most provocative dreams since she'd left him all those years ago.

As he worked the sander along the wood, the muscles in his arms and across his back bunched and shifted beneath the light blue cotton T-shirt he wore. The low slung waistband of his faded jeans clung to his lean hips and accentuated his toned butt and sinewy thighs. From what she could see, there wasn't an inch of excess on his well-built frame.

Caught up in the moment, Tess sighed dreamily. Atlanta, Georgia, the city where she now lived, just didn't grow men like this. Morgan was pure country, with a powerful body honed by hard physical labor—not from an expensive membership at the gym. And despite their years apart, he still had the ability to draw her like no other. Including Patrick O'Neal, the ex-fiancé she'd left behind in Atlanta when she'd made the decision to return to the small town of Wynhaven.

The last time she'd visited had been six months ago. It had been only a brief trip for her grandmother Helen's funeral before she'd returned to her life in Atlanta, which had quickly unraveled and fallen apart. Now she was back temporarily, to get her grandmother's big, run-down house ready to sell while she figured out what the heck she was going to do now that she was unemployed and unengaged.

Another few moments passed before Morgan finally switched off the piece of machinery and removed his protective goggles. He absently pushed his fingers through his pitch black hair, dislodging the sprinkling of sawdust clinging to the thick, rakishly long strands before he caressed that same hand over the lustrous slab of wood. His fingers traced the smooth lines and scalloped edge along the top of the piece, his touch slow and reverent, as if he were stroking a woman's curves instead.

An unexpected flood of memories swamped Tess, thrusting her back to when she was seventeen and the object of Morgan's affections. The sole focus of his warm, knowing touch. His exciting, adoring caresses. His deep, lush kisses that had seduced her into giving him her body and innocence that summer night long ago down by the lake next to her grandmother's house. Her stomach fluttered at the sensual recollection, and a soft moan escaped her before she could stop it.

Morgan turned around, obviously startled by the sound, as well as her unannounced appearance into his private domain. His piercing silver eyes locked on hers, and she caught a fleeting glimpse of surprise at seeing her. This was the first time she'd deliberately sought him out since their break-up so long ago. Then his gaze narrowed and he gave her an abrupt nod of his dark head as he eyed her with reserve.

"Tess," he murmured in that slow, lazy southern drawl that never failed to make her pulse race and a silky heat to spiral low. "I heard you were back in town."

And just that easily, all those regrets she'd buried after leaving him behind for a life in Atlanta—a life her grandmother had pushed her to pursue—came rushing back, making her stomach clench with remorse.

She hated that she'd caused Morgan any kind of pain, yet there was no way to take back her past actions. And there had been so many times she'd wished she'd made different choices, that she'd been strong and bold enough to do what her heart wanted, and not what had been expected of her.

Shoving those thoughts away, she summoned a smile, determined not to let Morgan's brusque attitude dissuade her. "I arrived a few days ago."

His brazen gaze drifted down the length of her body, visually stroking her full breasts and her long, slender legs before gradually making his way back up to her face again. Warmth pooled in her stomach as he lingered a few extra seconds on her mouth before lifting his eyes to hers again.

"You're looking . . . well," he said.

It wasn't much as far as greetings went, not that she'd been expecting some grand gesture like a welcoming hug, considering how strained things had grown between them over the past eight years. Now, he was reserved with her, and it pained her that they'd been reduced to this state of being polite and courteous with one another after everything they'd once shared. But she also knew she was mainly responsible for the emotional distance between them, and she hoped the gesture she was about to impart might help repair the damage she'd done to their relationship. That maybe this time around, when she returned to Atlanta, they could at least part ways as friends.

She shifted on her feet, gathering the confidence and composure that had served her well as a marketing rep for the large Atlanta firm she'd worked for. Before they'd decided to down-size and sent her on her way with a severance package that would help her through the next few months.

"Your secretary wasn't at your main office," she said, waving a hand toward the front of the building. "So I thought I'd follow the sounds coming from your workshop in hopes of finding you here."

His gaze turned wary as she stepped further into the shop and toward him, taking in the various woodworking pieces around the room. While Morgan had followed in his father's footsteps in becoming a jack-of-all-trades to the residents around Wynhaven, she'd heard that Morgan had expanded the company to include home and business restorations on a larger scale. It appeared he'd built Kane Construction into a successful venture.

And obviously, in his spare time it appeared he did what he'd always loved best. He worked with oak, creating and crafting exquisite, one-of-a-kind custom pieces of furniture that put manufactured designs to shame. The man was immensely talented when it came to his hands, and he'd always known just how to put them to good use.

"So, what brings you by, Tess?" he asked, bringing her attention back to him again.

His expression was cool, his stance equally standoffish, indicating that any attempt at pleasantries were now over. Which was just as well, because Morgan wasn't making any of this easy on her. Not that she had expected him to.

If Mr. Tough Guy wanted to keep things all business, she was fine with that. "I came by to hire you to do repair and carpentry work on my grandmother's house."

A quick burst of laughter escaped him. "You're kidding, right?"

"No." She frowned, taken aback by his skepticism. "My grandmother didn't take very good care of the place as you well know. It's a big house and more than she could ever handle on her own, and it needs a lot of work to get it back into decent shape."

He leaned his backside against a workbench, crossed his long legs at the ankles, and considered that for a moment. "And then what do you plan to do with the house?"

It was far too large for her to live in alone, and she didn't plan to stay in Wynhaven permanently. This was all a part of wrapping up those loose ends still dangling from her past. Her grandmother's house. Morgan. And discovering what she wanted out of life, without her grandmother's influence tugging at her conscience.

She shrugged. "I'll put it on the market and see what happens."

He folded his arms over his muscled chest and raised a dark brow. "While you go back to Atlanta and play?"

She blinked at his sarcasm and bristled. *"Play?"* she repeated, unable to keep the incredulity out of her tone. "Oh, yeah, Morgan, my life in Atlanta was one big party."

He glanced away and blew out a deep breath, as if he

knew he'd gone too far. But it gave her a good indication of just how much pain and resentment he still harbored toward her, and she hoped if he got a bit of that hurt off his chest they could go forward from there.

When his gaze returned to hers, his smoky eyes and expression were contrite. "I'm sorry. That was uncalled for," he said, his tone low and rough. "From what I've heard, you've done very well for yourself since leaving Wynhaven."

Which he'd probably learned through the grapevine. After all, her grandmother had been proud of her. She'd stressed the importance of a good education, a respectable job, and making a better life for herself than Tess's own mother had. And Tess had done her best to please the woman who'd raised her after Tess's mother had passed away, to make Helen Monroe proud where her own daughter had failed. Despite Helen's overbearing ideals, Tess had loved her grandmother dearly and felt as though she owed her at least that much for everything Helen had given up to take care of her.

"Not without a whole lot of hard work," she said, refusing to let Morgan think that anything about her life in Atlanta had been easy.

She'd worked two jobs while attending Georgia State University, and had taken on odd jobs to make ends meet. More times than she could count she'd foregone having extra food in her refrigerator in order to make her rent. And when she was so homesick she wanted to cry, she'd forced herself to go on, to get her bachelor's degree in business administration as she'd promised her grandmother she would.

But there wasn't a day that went by that she didn't think about the man she'd left behind in Wynhaven and how much she missed him. Especially in those dark lonely hours of the night when she lay awake in her bed and wished she'd never left the small, secure town in which she'd been raised. Or Morgan.

No amount of success had ever eased that misery, which told her just how much a hold this man still had on her heart and emotions. Even if she'd been banished from his.

She pushed her fingers through her hair, still unused to the short, sophisticated, shoulder-length style a coworker had talked her into getting a few months ago. "For the moment I'm unemployed," she told Morgan, not meeting his gaze. She wasn't proud of the fact that she'd been one of the reps the firm had chosen to lay off, even though it had been a logical choice since she'd had the least seniority in the company. "Which gives me the free time to finally settle the issue of fixing up my grandmother's house and getting it sold."

She forced herself to look at him again. "So, what I need to know is if your company is available to do the repairs and restoration work."

He shook his head, though there was no regret in the gesture, or his expression. "Sorry. My guys are all in the middle of different jobs and I don't have anyone to spare right now."

"And you?" she ventured boldly.

A faint smile twisted the corner of his lips. "I'm not interested." *In taking on the job, or you,* his tone all but implied.

She kept her disappointment to herself. "I understand."

And she truly did. She knew his reasons for declining had nothing to do with business, but was based on their past and all the personal heartbreak between them. He had no desire to do *anything* for her. Business or otherwise.

Judging by his unrelenting expression, the man was adamant about his decision, and she silently admitted defeat. "I heard that Wayne Zimmerman down at the lumber mill does handyman work on the side. I'll go by there tomorrow and see if he can't help me out with what I need."

A muscle in Morgan's lean jaw clenched, the only show of emotion he allowed. "You do that," he drawled.

Knowing there was nothing left to say between them, she smiled and took a step back, prepared to go. "It was nice seeing you again, Morgan."

"Yeah, you, too," he said, his voice low and husky.

For a moment, she could have sworn she'd seen a flicker of longing pass over his features. Then it was gone, leaving her to wonder if she'd imagined the sentiment. Which she probably had.

Without another word, she turned and walked out of his workshop. Minutes later she was in her Honda Accord, heading back to her grandmother's big, lonely house and all the work that awaited her.

* * *

Morgan sat sprawled on a cushioned wicker chair out on his front porch in the complete darkness, nursing a cold bottle of beer as he stared up at the clear, star-studded sky. The summer evening was warm, increasing the scent of pine in the air, while crickets chirped in the distance. Normally he found the ritual soothing, but to-night there was no relaxation to be found.

He couldn't get Tess and her visit out of his mind, and Lord knew he'd tried. After work he'd headed off to a bar he frequented in a nearby town when he was looking to have a good time—and tonight he'd been looking to release a whole lot of tension. Mentally and physically.

The opportunity had presented itself in Wendy Lan-ders, an aggressive redhead with whom he'd slept a few times before. Their casual affair was all about pleasure and satisfaction—both of them lived by the no-strings-attached philosophy, which had suited him just fine. But despite how determined Wendy had been about her in-tentions with him tonight, he hadn't been able to drum up the enthusiasm to take advantage of what she'd freely offered him.

And that had royally pissed him off. He was a red-blooded guy who liked sex. He enjoyed every aspect of being with a warm, willing woman, from foreplay to cli-max to the physical gratification that came from a good, hard fuck. But it appeared Tess had turned him into a monk for the evening, because no matter how hard he'd tried to make it happen between him and Wendy, his body had refused to rise to the occasion.

"Shit," he muttered, and took a long pull of his beer,

aggravated to no end that Tess had ruined what should have been a great Friday night.

With a low growl, he leaned his head back against the chair and closed his eyes. Big mistake, he realized, as visions of her came into focus. Tired of fighting her allure, he allowed the images to come into sharp focus in his mind and saw her as she'd been in his workshop today.

God, she'd turned into a beautiful, sensual woman—from being a slender, willowy teenage girl to a twenty-six-year-old female with full breasts, lush curves, and a firm looking ass that swayed enticingly when she walked.

Her face had definitely matured over the years. Where her features had once been cute and pretty, she now possessed a radiance and beauty and sophistication—a noticeable contrast to most of the women who lived in Wynhaven.

He wasn't sure about her hair, though, he thought with a frown. He'd always loved it long, loved the way her hair draped halfway down her back and how he'd been able to wrap those thick blond strands around his fists in the throes of passion. Now she wore it in a short sleek style that barely brushed her shoulders, though he had to admit that the citified look suited her and went with the rest of her trendy packaging.

Her eyes were still as brown and expressive as he remembered, her mouth just as tempting. Oh, yeah, she'd been so damn eager to learn what turned him on and had done things to him with that sweet mouth of hers that had shattered his control and blown his mind.

Even now, his body recalled how her soft lips and

warm, wet tongue had pleasured him. A rush of heat settled in his groin, making him hard as a spike, and he
groaned at the irony of it. While he was grateful to know
he could still get it up after his lack of interest in Wendy,
he was aggravated that Tess still had the ability to affect
him so easily. He would have thought after eight years
and many women, his past relationship with Tess would
be a distant memory. Unfortunately, the recollection of
their time together was still fresh and vivid in his mind.

As was the devastating choice she'd made soon after
she'd graduated high school.

Tess's mother had died when she was eight, and without knowing who her father was her grandmother had
raised her on her own. Helen had never made a secret of
her disapproval of Morgan or their relationship because
she'd never seen Morgan as someone who was good
enough for her granddaughter, yet he'd foolishly believed that he and Tess would continue seeing one another while she attended college and he stayed in
Wynhaven to take over his father's business.

He'd thought wrong.

Instead, she'd ended their relationship, telling him
that she needed more than what Wynhaven had to offer,
that this was her chance to make a better life for herself—as if she'd agreed with her grandmother and decided he wasn't good enough for her.

Then she'd taken off for Atlanta, leaving him and the
small town behind to pursue her dreams without him.

The rejection had stung, especially since he'd believed his future was right here in Wynhaven with Tess. She'd been his first love, and so far, his last.

God, what a complete and total sap he'd been!

Feeling restless, he stood, walked to the end of the porch, and braced his hands on the wooden rail. He stared out at the shadowed darkness beyond his front yard, wondering what the hell he was going to do now that Tess was back in town. He'd been doing just fine all these years without her, and after one brief encounter he was tied up in knots over her once again.

She'd made it clear she was going to be around for a good month or so to repair her grandmother's house and put it on the market. She needed help with the work, and after he'd refused her request she'd suggested using Wayne Zimmerman.

He cursed beneath his breath. The cold hard truth was, he didn't want any other guy, especially a known womanizer like Wayne, around Tess on a daily basis. Not when Morgan still wanted her, and not when there were so many unresolved feelings where Tess was concerned. And he knew nothing short of having her again would do.

If anyone would be seducing Tess Monroe, he decided, it would be *him*.

Instead of living the next month in pure frustration, he was going to help Tess restore her grandmother's house and coax her back into his bed at the same time— a temporary, mutually pleasurable affair guaranteed to satisfy them both. Eight years was way too long to let a woman have a hold over him. This was his chance to finally get her out of his mind and heart once and for all, and be the one to walk away with his emotions intact this time.

Now all he had to do was put his plan into motion, which he'd do first thing tomorrow morning, before she had a chance to talk to Wayne.

CHAPTER ◆ TWO

Tess reached up and plucked another ripe peach from one of the trees behind her grandmother's house and put it into the bowl she held in the crook of her arm. It was only eight in the morning, the grass still wet with dew, and the air redolent with the sweet scent of peaches and the promise of the warm, humid summer day ahead.

She'd woken up that morning craving peach pancakes for breakfast, just like her grandmother used to make for her. How great was it that she could step outside and pick the fresh fruit right from its tree? That was something she couldn't have done from her small apartment in Atlanta, and the peaches at the market just hadn't been as sweet and juicy as these grown at home.

Since the house had been vacant and the yard untouched for the past six months, the trees were abundant with plump, juicy peaches, and the ground littered with the spoiled produce. She'd have to get that cleaned up at some point as well.

Her stomach growled hungrily, and she smiled and grabbed another peach from a high branch, thinking maybe later, after she got some work done around the house, she'd make peach jam or cobbler and take some with her when she went to go talk to Wayne. There was certainly plenty of the fruit for her to make enough jam for the entire town if she wanted.

With her bowl filled, she stepped back to retreat to the house, and something beneath the sole of her fluffy house slipper popped then squished under her foot—the third one this morning. She cringed, knowing she'd just stomped on yet another over-ripe peach. "Oh, ugh!"

Deep male laughter sounded from behind her, brushing down her spine like a seductive caress. Startled, she spun around and almost dropped the bowl of peaches, which she quickly steadied against her arm. She found Morgan leaning casually against the side of the house, his thumbs hooked into the belt loop of his jeans as he watched her with an amused expression on his face. How long he'd been there, she hadn't a clue. But now she knew how it felt to be spied on, just as she'd spied on him yesterday before announcing her presence.

He continued to stare at her, one of those sexy, lopsided smiles of his tugging at the corners of his mouth as his gaze slowly slid from her disheveled hair all the way down to her fuzzy psychedelic slippers, then back up again.

A flash of heat zinged across her nerve endings,

along with a ripple of shocking awareness. Her breasts swelled and her nipples puckered in reaction to his hot stare, and it was all she could do not to fold her arms across her chest to hide that telltale response.

She hadn't been expecting company and was still wearing what she'd slept in—a pair of pink and purple plaid boxer shorts and a ribbed tank top that was made for comfort, and not to conceal her curves and erect nipples.

She started toward him, careful not to step on any more rotten peach bombs on her way. "Morgan," she said, her tone as cautious as she felt. "What are you doing here?"

"I've reconsidered your request about hiring me to do the work around here," he said, his eyes a warm, mellow shade of gray this morning—unlike the cool silver she'd encountered at his workshop yesterday.

What an interesting turn of events, she thought, curious to know what had changed his mind. Especially after his gruff reception with her the day before. But she wasn't about to refuse his help, and she nodded toward the back door to the house. "How about we go inside and talk?"

He nodded, causing a dark lock of hair to fall across his forehead. For a moment he reminded her of the bad boy she'd fallen in love with—until she remembered just how much of a man he'd become. But she didn't doubt that he still had a reckless streak beneath all that maturity.

"That works for me," he said easily, and followed her inside.

The door led into the kitchen, and she set the bowl of
fruit on the Formica counter, which was old and cracked
in places—one of the many items she needed to replace.
"I was going to make myself some peach pancakes," she
said as she turned to face him again. "Would you like
some?"

She fully expected him to say no to her polite offer, to
tell her he was there for business and nothing more, but he
went and threw her another curve she wasn't anticipating.

"That sounds great." He gave his rock-hard stomach
a pat. "I'm starved."

The low, rumbling way he said the word *starved,* cou-
pled with the hungry way he continued to stare at her,
made her feel as though he were contemplating *her* for
breakfast. She shivered at the thought. If he was trying
to throw her off balance, he was doing a damn good job
of it.

The kitchen was fairly spacious with a sturdy wooden
table off to the side of the room, but with Morgan standing only a few feet away it seemed to shrink in size.
Again, she became aware of her skimpy attire and knew
she wouldn't be able to carry on a conversation dressed
as she was, and with his bold gaze admiring her breasts.

"I'm going to run upstairs and change," she said as
she moved toward the doorway leading to the other
rooms in the house. "I'll be right back. There's fresh
coffee in the pot, so help yourself."

With a hand on her jittery stomach, she jogged up the
stairs to the upper landing and the room she'd been
given when she'd come to live here permanently after

her mother had been killed in a car crash with her boyfriend. The master bedroom was down the hall and much larger with a connecting bathroom, but Tess hadn't been able to bring herself to move into what had been her grandmother's room. She still missed her grandmother, and there were just too many memories still lingering in her bedroom. Besides, she wasn't going to be in Wynhaven long, anyway, so she'd rather stay where it was cozy and familiar.

She changed into a pair of soft worn jeans and a loose Georgia State University T-shirt, ran a brush through her hair to restore order to the tousled strands, and returned to the kitchen in less than ten minutes. She found Morgan standing by the sink, in the process of peeling the skin from the peaches. Two steaming mugs of coffee sat on the counter next to him.

He looked perfectly at home in *her* home, and she wasn't sure what to make of it . . . or where all this niceness was coming from or leading.

Heading to the counter next to him, she poured cream into one of the mugs of coffee and stirred in a spoonful of sugar. "You don't need to peel the peaches for me. I can do it." She took a sip of her coffee, certain she needed the kick of caffeine to help bolster her fortitude for whatever was to come.

"It's not a big deal." He rinsed another ripe fruit then dragged the sharp knife along the surface, quickly and efficiently paring the peach and making good use of those capable hands of his. He placed the denuded piece of fruit into a colander and grinned at her. "I just thought I'd help you get started on those pancakes."

She gathered the ingredients she needed for the batter, all the while contemplating the best way to approach Morgan about his impromptu visit. Just get right to the point, she supposed.

And so she did. "What's going on, Morgan?" she asked as she measured out the flour, baking powder, and sugar into a big mixing bowl. "Yesterday you didn't want to have anything to do with me and today you're Mr. Hospitality. And don't give me any crap about being neighborly, because I'm just not buying it."

He chuckled at her outspoken manner and began chopping the peaches into small pieces for the batter. "Don't sugarcoat things on my account, sweetheart."

That endearment . . . God, coming from him, in that lazy, sexy drawl he'd once used to coax her into letting him do sinful things to her—with her. It still had the ability to make her weak in the knees, and damp in secret places. He'd always been able to seduce her with his voice and words alone, and he hadn't lost the ability to do so now.

"I guess I'm just not the genteel, Southern girl I used to be," she replied with a bit of impudence as she whipped the rest of the ingredients together in quick, frenzied motion. "So, quit beating around the bush with your reasons for being here."

"Alright," he said, his tone and features turning serious. Finished slicing up the fruit, he washed his hands and dried them with a terrycloth towel. "I came here to offer a truce, and my restoration services."

She gently folded the peaches into the batter and slanted him a sideways glance, trying not to let her relief show. She was grateful that he was willing to put aside the estrangement between them, but she suspected there was more to this friendly reconciliation than he was letting on.

Still, she wasn't about to turn away such an unexpected and welcome gift. "Truce accepted."

"And my services?" Reaching for his coffee, he watched her over the rim of the mug as he took a drink.

She dropped a slab of butter into the hot skillet on the stove and waited for it to melt. "Depends on why you changed your mind."

He shrugged. "It's a job, and money is money, no matter who it comes from. My father always taught me not to discriminate, so I guess I shouldn't start now."

She couldn't stop the smile that eased across her lips. "Your father always was a smart man." Mr. Kane had also been hardworking, openly affectionate with his family, always kind to her, and someone she would have loved to call her own father. Especially since she'd never known her own dad and still felt that empty sense of loss even now that she was a grown adult.

Scooping up a cup of batter, she poured it into the sizzling frying pan, making two large, separate pancakes. "So, this is a business decision then?"

"And a personal one," he admitted, but didn't elaborate on that. "I figure the sooner I help you knock out the work on this place, the sooner you can return to Atlanta and do your thing."

"You mean *play?*" she said, teasing him.

Returning her humorous grin, he leaned his hip against the counter and slid the fingers of one hand into the front pocket of his jeans. "I was thinking more along the lines of you finding another job."

A sigh unraveled out of her as she turned over the flapjacks. The tops were brown, buttery, crispy, and smelled heavenly—just like her grandmother taught her to make them. "Yeah, there is that." She wasn't looking forward to getting back to that nine-to-five grind, the hectic pace, the traffic, the stress of having to work against tight deadlines. "I certainly can't live on my severance and savings forever."

"I'm sure the money from the sale of this place will help you out."

"Yes, it will." She was lucky that the house was paid for, which meant a huge sum of money for her, a nest egg that would go a long way in helping her to move out of her apartment in Atlanta and finally buy a house of her own. That was her plan, anyway.

He set aside his coffee mug. "So, what can I do to help?"

"You can set the table while I finish making the pancakes." She pointed her spatula toward the cupboard behind him. "The dishes and silverware are still in the same place."

With a nod, he gathered the plates and utensils and put them on the table, then the butter and syrup from the refrigerator. He hadn't eaten there often, just when her grandmother wasn't around, but he had no problem finding whatever they needed for breakfast now. Whereas his parents had always treated her like one of their own kids, Helen Monroe never did embrace Morgan or Tess's relationship with him. They had had to sneak around to be together, even though her grandmother had been smart enough to figure out what was going on behind her back and made sure Tess knew her feelings on Morgan Kane: that he was wild and reckless and pure trouble, and if she wasn't careful Tess was going to end up like her mother. Knocked up and on her own, with no way to support herself and her child.

The pain of those words still had the ability to pierce Tess's heart. She never believed that Morgan would ever do to her what Tess's own father had done to her mother. But at the age of eighteen, with her grandmother pushing her to make something of her life outside of Wynhaven, Tess had not only been conflicted and confused, but she'd felt an obligation to her grandmother after everything she'd sacrificed for her.

And where had any of it gotten her? Educated beyond high school, yes, and working a well-paying job, and getting engaged to the right kind of man by her grandmother's standards, but she'd given up so much in exchange for that distinction. Important, deeply meaningful things she might not ever be able to reclaim because of the emotional damage she'd inflicted on the one person who'd meant so much to her as a result of the choices she'd made.

She harbored a wealth of regrets about the past and her actions, but she couldn't change any of it. All she could do now was be true to what was in her heart and see where it led her now.

Once she finished the peach pancakes, she brought them to the table on a big platter while Morgan refilled their coffee mugs. They sat down across from one another and dug in, with Morgan piling four of the flapjacks onto his plate while she took just one. After buttering the pancakes and pouring syrup over them, he took a few bites of the peach confection and groaned his appreciation.

He swiped his napkin across his mouth and glanced across the table at her, a playful gleam in his eyes. "I'm glad to see you haven't forgotten how to cook."

She raised a brow, more amused than offended by his comment. "Now what's that supposed to mean?"

"Being a working girl, I'm sure it was easier to grab something on the run, or put a frozen meal into the microwave." He popped another big bite of pancake into his mouth and was already slicing into another section to eat.

"It *was* easier," she admitted and took a drink of her coffee. "And it isn't much fun cooking for one person." As for Patrick, he'd preferred to eat at his favorite five-star restaurants around town where his lawyer father had open accounts for him to use.

She watched Morgan devour the rest of the pancakes on his plate and take the last two from the platter. She shook her head as she took a dainty bite of her own breakfast, near to being stuffed on just one flapjack. The man's appetite amazed her, but she was pleased that he was enjoying the meal so much. It *was* nice to know she hadn't lost her touch in the kitchen, because she'd always loved to cook. Missed it, actually.

"You'd better be careful how much you eat or you're going to go soft around the middle," she said, just to tease him.

He raised his smoky gray eyes to hers and grinned rakishly. "Don't worry about me, sweetheart, I burn off plenty of calories to make up for how much I eat."

He followed that up with a waggle of those dark brows of his, insinuating something of the sexual variety. Her pulse leapt and she glanced back down at her own breakfast. She wasn't going to touch that statement, because her fertile imagination was doing just fine on its own without him adding more fuel to that fire.

"How's your sister doing?" she asked, as much to change the subject as to find out how Amy had fared in the eight years that had passed between them. Amy had been her best friend growing up, even after Tess had fallen hard for her older brother.

"She's still happily married to Jake Barber with two adorable but rambunctious little boys. Todd is six, and Gavin is four, and she's pregnant with number three. They're hoping for a girl this time."

"That's so great." As young girls, she and Amy had

always talked about getting married and having kids, and being a wife and mother. It was what they'd both wanted, and at least one of them had achieved her dreams. To pursue her grandmother's wishes, Tess had given up hers, along with the man sitting in front of her with whom she'd wanted to have those babies.

She set her fork on her plate and pushed it aside. "I've missed her friendship." She couldn't help the wistful quality of her voice.

Morgan stopped eating and raised his eyes to hers. "I know she missed you, too, Tess. You were her best friend."

That was yet another regret to bear, and one she wanted to mend. A lump rose in the back of Tess's throat and she swallowed it back. "When I left . . . after the way you and I parted ways, well, I didn't think she'd ever want to speak to me again."

"I won't lie to you, Tess. Amy was pretty upset at first, mostly on my behalf, but I know over the years she wished that things had ended differently between the two of you." Then he did the unexpected and reached across the table, placed his hand over hers, and gave it an encouraging squeeze. "Look at it this way. I'm speaking to you again, so there's hope for my sister, too."

His sincerity was unmistakable, the warmth of his touch oddly comforting. "I'd like to think that your sister might come around." She withdrew her hand from his, stood, and stacked the empty plates and utensils. "Since I'm going to be in town for a while, I'll stop by her place sometime and say hello."

"I'm sure she'd like that." After finishing his coffee, he stood, too, and helped her clear the table. Once that was done and she was rinsing everything to put into the dishwasher, he said, "I'm going to go get my estimate pad from my truck and we can get to business."

She nodded as she scrubbed the skillet clean. "Sounds good."

He returned minutes later, just as she was closing up the dishwasher. She rinsed her hands, wiped them on a dry towel, and turned around to face him. He held a clipboard in his hand with what looked like an invoice attached, and he was writing her name and the address of the house in the top half of the sheet.

He was back to being all business, their earlier moment of bonding over with. "How do you want to handle this?" she asked.

Finished writing, he tucked the pencil behind his ear. "First we'll go through the house together and make a list of what needs to be done, and from there I can give you an estimate of what it's going to cost."

She pushed her fingers into the back pockets of her jeans. "Fair enough."

He glanced around the room, his gaze scrutinizing everything from the ceiling to the floor and everything in between. "Let's start here in the kitchen, head outside to see what needs to be done there, then work our way up to the second level."

She stated the obvious problems in the kitchen. "The linoleum and Formica countertops are cracked and torn and need to be redone, and that back screen door is rotting around the hinges, so I'd like to get that replaced, too."

"That's easy enough." He measured the length of the countertops, jotted down the figures on his estimate sheet, then squatted down and peeled back a corner of the old linoleum covering the floor. "You've got hardwood floors beneath all this. If you had them refinished, it would match beautifully with the rest of the downstairs."

She was surprised to find out that her grandmother had covered up the beautiful wood. "That would look great."

From there, they headed out the back door and assessed the damage on the outside of the house. Morgan told her he'd hire some teenage boys to clean up the yard and rotten peaches, and plant a few roses bushes around the front to make the place more appealing to the eye of a prospective buyer. The planks along the porch needed to be replaced, along with the front stairs that threatened to collapse beneath Morgan's weight. The old, cracked and peeling paint on the house and along the trim needed to be sanded and restored to its former luster and beauty.

Back inside, they went from room to room, noting problems and concerns, which included a new banister, the plumbing in the third bathroom upstairs that was leaking, a few electrical issues, and ancient light fixtures that needed to be upgraded. Just like the outside of the house, he told her that a fresh coat of paint would go a long way in brightening up the interior of the house and make it more inviting.

Lastly, they ended up in her bedroom, and with Morgan standing close beside her she was swamped with instantaneous awareness and provocative memories of the times the two of them had made love on her bed. Her mind conjured up the way they'd looked together, with her legs wrapped tight around his hips, her fingers digging into the muscled flesh along his back, and her body eager and straining beneath the heat and hardness of his.

She cleared her throat before one of those telltale groans could escape and give Morgan too much insight into her lustful thoughts, and walked to the bedroom window. She unlatched it and gave it a tug, but it wouldn't budge.

She released a frustrated sigh. "This window is stuck and won't open, no matter how hard I try. It would be nice to get it to work again so I can have some fresh air at night."

He tossed his clipboard on the bed before coming up next to her and giving it a hard, upward jerk. With a crackling, peeling sound the wooden casing came loose and separated from the frame, allowing the window to open about a foot and a half before it came to a stop again.

She rolled her eyes. It figured he'd be able to open it so effortlessly after she'd been struggling for days to do it on her own. "I guess those muscles of yours come in handy after all, don't they?"

He just laughed as he examined the tracking along the sides of the window. "It looks like the wood around the frame has swelled from dampness and rain and not being used often enough. A bit of shaving and resealing along the edges ought to make it as good as new."

He leaned out the window to check the condition of the outer frame, and when he came back inside he was chuckling.

"What's so funny?" she asked, unable to figure out what he'd found so entertaining.

He shook his head, though there was a wicked gleam in his eyes. "Nothing."

She didn't believe him. "It was obviously *something*."

He propped his hands on his waist and hesitated a moment before sharing what had amused him. "Remember the time we ditched school and spent the day up here in your room?"

A quiver surged through her. Oh, yeah, she remembered vividly. With her grandmother spending the day with a friend shopping in Atlanta, it had been an afternoon indulging in sexual decadence and forbidden pleasures for her and Morgan.

Still, she didn't get the joke. "And you find that memory funny?"

"No, I find it damn arousing," he said, his drawl deep and rich and seductive. "But what we did up here together wasn't what I was laughing at. I was thinking about how your grandmother came home earlier than you'd expected and when we heard her calling your name from downstairs you completely panicked."

Her eyes widened as the recollection poured through her mind, thrusting her back into the past. Fearful of what would happen if her grandmother found her and

Morgan together, she'd pushed him out of her bed, whispering frantically for him to put on his clothes and go while she'd tossed on her own blouse and shorts. But the only way out of the room without getting caught was the window, and they both knew that was the exit he'd have to take.

When her grandmother's voice echoed up the stairway, Tess had pushed a half-dressed Morgan toward the window and shoved him out, hoping to God that he'd be able to use the trellis along the side of the house to help him get down to the ground safely. But that hadn't happened at all.

A giggle bubbled up into her throat, and she clapped her hand over her mouth to keep it contained.

"Go ahead and laugh." His eyes danced with the same humor tickling through her. "You didn't even give me the chance to get my pants up around my hips before you were jamming me through the window as fast as you could. So, with my bare ass half hanging out of my jeans, I lost my grip and fell into the flower bed and nearly broke my neck."

She was laughing now, a deep throated chuckle that matched his. The whole scenario was hysterically funny now, but at the time she remembered the horror of watching him fall two stories down. He'd landed on his side, crawled out of the flower bed, and with a grimace of pain he'd waved at her that he was okay before fleeing the back way toward his parents' house.

As for her, she'd had just enough time to grab a school math book, plop herself back onto her bed, and pretend that she'd fallen asleep while doing homework before her grandmother had opened the door to her room to check on her.

Once her mirth subsided, she wiped the moisture from her eyes. "Oh, God, Morgan, what were we thinking to take that chance fooling around up here that day?"

"I don't think either of us were thinking." Lifting his hand, he gently brushed the tips of his fingers along her smooth cheek, then cradled the side of her face in his large palm. "We were *feeling* all kinds of good stuff, and we lost track of time."

All traces of laughter and amusement between them faded at that moment. Her face warmed beneath his touch, and she felt herself falling, spiraling straight into the kind of desire and need she hadn't felt in so, so long.

His gaze locked on hers, and she watched, fascinated, as his eyes darkened and turned to slate. She knew that hot, sexy look of his that reminded her of a male alpha wolf on the prowl. Remembered it well. And it obviously still had the power to delight and excite her.

"Morgan, what are you doing?" Her voice was a croak of sound.

"I believe I'm about to mix business with a little pleasure." His thumb skimmed across her bottom lip, tugging it open ever so slightly. "The moment I saw you in my workshop yesterday I wanted to kiss you, and since we'll be working so closely together and I'm constantly distracted by thoughts of kissing you, I figure we might as well get it out of the way now." He stepped closer, bringing with him an earthy, elemental scent that made her dizzy with want for him. "Do you have a problem with that, sweetheart?"

Her mind told her to tell him *yes,* she had a huge problem with him putting his lips on hers, because she knew how lost she'd be once he did so. Their business deal didn't include the kind of pleasure his eyes were promising, but she had intimate knowledge of just how well this man could kiss.

Slow and thorough, and just wet enough to electrify every one of her feminine senses. Soft, deeply erotic kisses that gradually escalated into a fierce and urgent hunger.

His irresistible kisses had been the ones she'd judged all others by—and found each one lacking in comparison.

Her heart beat erratically in her chest. Her breathing deepened, and she had to swallow hard to speak. "No, I don't have a problem with that. Not at all."

"Good," he said, and finally lowered his mouth to hers.

CHAPTER ◆ THREE

As soon as Morgan's lips touched Tess's, hers parted in invitation, but he was in no rush to complete this kiss. He had eight long years to make up for in this one moment, and he planned to do his damndest to make it good . . . for both of them.

Nibbling lightly at her plump bottom lip, he maneuvered her back a few steps, until she was up against the wall next to the window. He slid a hand into her hair, enjoying the feel of the silky textured strands sliding through his fingers, and he cupped the back of her head in his palm, which gave him control over just how deep and how long he planned to kiss her.

He started out slow, relearning the feel of her lips against his, and when she let out a shivery sigh he slid his tongue lazily inside her warm, welcoming mouth.

While he was reacquainting himself with the sweet, hot taste that was Tess, she was busy running her hands down his chest. Then she caught her fingers in the waistband of his jeans, pulled him close, and moved her pelvis sensuously against his.

A burning ache settled in his groin. Sweeping his other hand down to her bottom, he grabbed her ass and lifted her higher, tighter, against him. He fit the length of his erection between her parted thighs and rolled his hips just as aggressively. She gasped and shuddered, and he swallowed the sound as his tongue delved deeper, the kiss grew wetter, wilder, and their bodies strained and ignited like wildfire.

God, she was still just as passionate as she'd been at seventeen, if not more so. Just as eager and responsive. And he went a little bit crazy thinking about how incredible it would feel to be inside her again. To have his hands all over her sleek, naked flesh, his cock buried deep, and his mouth on her full, lush breasts.

His control threatened to snap, and with a low growl he pulled his mouth from hers before he pushed her down on the nearby bed, ripped off their clothes, and followed through on his carnal thoughts.

Flattening his hands on either side of her head, he moved back just enough so that he no longer had her pinned against the wall and they both had a bit more breathing room.

"That was nice," he murmured against her ear. "Very nice."

"Mmmm," she hummed, which was all she seemed to be able to manage.

He glanced down at her, taking in her dazed expression, the hair that was mussed from his hands, her soft, kiss-swollen lips, and thought she looked like sex personified. "You always were a hot little thing. It's nice to know that hasn't changed."

Her eyes flashed indignantly, clearing out the fog of desire clouding the depths. "And you always were much too cocky for your own good. It appears you still are."

He grinned, liking this strong, impertinence she'd developed over the years. "Only when it comes to something I'm confident about."

Her chin lifted a fraction, as did a brow. "And what would that be?"

"You. This. Us." He slipped his hand beneath the hem of her T-shirt, let it rest heavily on the curve of her waist, and stroked his thumb along the bare, silken flesh above the waistband of her jeans.

She sucked in a quick, startled breath.

He grinned triumphantly. "It's still there, isn't it?"

She blinked up at him, obviously trying to pretend that his touch no longer had the ability to make her melt and bend to his will. "What's still there?"

She was feigning ignorance by playing dumb, and he decided to up the stakes between them. His palm slid higher, until his fingers feathered beneath her breast, making her gulp back a low moan that managed to escape her throat anyway.

"The chemistry, the heat," he said, and because she'd felt how much he'd wanted her just minutes ago, he added, "The need for me to get as deep inside you as possible."

A low gust of breath unraveled out of her, though much to his surprise she managed to remain outwardly composed. "You think I'm that easy?"

"Easy?" he repeated, then shook his head. "Hell, no. A grown woman with desires and sexual needs? Absolutely."

The corner of her mouth tipped up in a derisive smile. "And you think you're just the man to take care of those needs, right?"

He skimmed his fingers back down to her flat belly and felt goose bumps rise on her flesh. "What I know is how good it was between us eight years ago, and how good it feels now. So why not enjoy?"

She stared at him for a long moment, as if trying to figure out his angle . . . and if he was truly serious about his intentions. "So, if I hire you, does that mean you're going to spend the next month trying to get inside my pants?"

He laughed, the sound brimming with amusement. "You know me, Tess. I always did love a good challenge. But the way I see things, the only way I can get into your pants is if you let me." Because for as much as he still wanted her, it was ultimately up to Tess to surrender to him of her own free will.

With that, he moved away from her and picked up his

clipboard from her bed, ready to be on his way and leave her with her own thoughts about what *she* wanted. At the door, he stopped and glanced back at Tess, her bewildered expression telling him she wasn't sure what to make of what had just transpired between them.

He liked seeing her a little off-balance, and knew the next few weeks were going to be very interesting, indeed.

"Thanks for breakfast," he said appreciatively. "I'll have an estimate for you by tomorrow, and I can get started on the restoration work on Monday."

She nodded mutely, still standing against the wall across the room from him.

He grinned, winked at her, and then he was gone.

Tess glanced out the kitchen window to the back-yard as she placed half a dozen of the peach cobbler cookies she'd baked earlier that morning on a plate, and smiled at the transformation she saw.

For the past five days the three high-school boys Morgan had hired to do the yard work had labored long and hard to get the outside of the place back into shape. Overgrown weeds had been pulled and the debris removed, and the lawn had been mowed and fertilized, giving it a well-manicured look.

The ground beneath the peach trees had been cleared of rotten fruit and the branches and leaves had been neatly trimmed back. The trees now looked healthy and less burdened by overripe peaches, though there was still an abundance to pick from, which accounted for all the baking and recipes Tess had been experimenting with over the past few days.

Retrieving a pitcher from the refrigerator, she filled a large plastic tumbler with the iced tea, amazed at how much had been accomplished in a week and a half's time. Despite Morgan's initial claim that he didn't have any men to spare for the restoration work, he'd managed to bring in a small crew of three of his guys to help him with the more time-consuming chores. As a result, the outside of the house was nearly restored to a dazzling, beautiful sight—from a new coat of paint that made the structure look a good twenty years younger than it really was, to the thriving plants and shrubs and blooming flowers around the perimeter of the house that added a new stately, elegant dimension to the two-story residence.

Morgan still had the inside to refurbish, but it was apparent that the once run-down house was gradually coming to life and taking on a personality all of its own. And so was something within Tess: a bubbling excitement and an inexplicable optimism for the future that she'd yet to fully define.

Picking up the plate of cookies and the iced tea, Tess headed out the kitchen's back door and followed the sound of steady hammering to the front of the house, where Morgan had spent the better part of the day working to replace the porch floorboards and stairs.

As she rounded the last corner, she met with the gorgeous, breathtaking sight of Morgan without his shirt on. His worn and faded jeans rode low on his hips from the leather tool belt secured around his waist, and the muscles across his broad back rippled and flexed as he wielded the hammer with expertise. His hair was damp with perspiration, as was all of that glorious, bare and tanned skin of his.

Her stomach fluttered with awareness, and her hands itched to touch all that hot, slick flesh, to feel his strong, hard body beneath her fingertips—every single inch of him.

As much as she hated to admit it, especially to herself, she was falling under Morgan's spell. True to his word, he'd spent the past week flirting shamelessly with her, and when they were alone he wasn't shy about stealing more of those hot, provocative kisses from her. So, by the time she crawled into bed at night, her body was tight and achy and she had the most vivid, erotic dreams of the two of them together that left her restless and wanting. Just as he'd no doubt intended, the rogue!

He was building the sexual tension between them to a fever pitch, and she was actually enjoying the seduction more than was wise. The man was just so damn charming and sexy, and it had been so long since she'd felt so feminine and desirable.

"Hey there," she said, just as he straightened after nailing down another floorboard. "I brought you a cool drink and a snack. Everybody has already left for the day, and I thought you could use a break."

He glanced her way and swiped the back of his forearm across his damp forehead. "I want to get this finished today."

"You're almost done." She set the plastic tumbler and plate on the sturdy new stairs, sat down, and indicated the space next to her. "Come and rest for a few minutes and I'll leave you alone again. I promise."

His gaze took in the treat she'd brought for him, and seemingly unable to resist, he slipped his hammer into his tool belt and sat down beside her. She couldn't help but notice the way he spread his long legs in an inherently masculine position, or the way the denim stretched taut across his muscled thighs.

She handed him the iced tea, and he downed half of the contents in a single gulp. Then he picked up a peach cobbler cookie and tossed the entire thing into his mouth and chewed.

He groaned his enjoyment of the confection and filched another. "Damn but those are good. I hope you made extra for me to take home."

His eyes sparkled mischievously and she laughed. She'd gotten into the habit of sending him home with a care package of whatever she'd baked that day. "I'm thinking that you're getting way too spoiled."

An unapologetic grin curved his mouth. "It's your own fault for baking all this great stuff."

"What else am I supposed to do with all those ripe peaches? I hate to let them go to waste."

"Trust me, I'm not complaining. After all, I'm reaping the benefits of all your experimenting." He ate another moist cookie and took a drink of his tea. "You know, I do have to say, you'd make a fortune if you ever decided to sell your baked goods."

She rolled her eyes at that. "I don't think opening a bakery in Atlanta is my calling."

His curious gaze met hers. "What *are* you going to do once you go back?"

She glanced out at the yard and sighed, wishing she had a solid answer to his question, but she didn't. Her life at the moment was in limbo even though she still had her apartment in Atlanta under lease.

"I honestly don't know," she told him. "I've got a degree in business administration and I've had a few years experience as a marketing rep, so I suppose that's my logical choice of employment." And although getting another job was inevitable, she realized she was in no hurry to return to that stressful rat race.

He cast her a quizzical look. "Did you enjoy what you did for a living?"

She shrugged and brushed back a strand of hair tickling her cheek. "It was a job."

"But not something you loved," he stated, guessing at her unspoken thoughts.

It amazed her that he could still read her so well, even after all these years. "Not in the way you love what you do."

Abrupt laughter escaped him. "Trust me, there are days that this job sucks."

Resting her elbows on her knees, she propped her chin in her hand and smiled at him. "Do you ever feel that way about your woodwork?"

"Can't say that I do." He finished off the last cookie and the rest of his iced tea. "Being in my workshop and shaping a slab of oak into a piece of custom-made furniture is my way of relaxing after a long day at work. It's like therapy for me."

"I'd love to find something like that." There was a wistful quality to her voice she couldn't hold back.

"You seem pretty happy and relaxed in the kitchen when you're baking," he pointed out.

"It's a nice hobby, but it's not going to support me or pay bills. I'm just lucky that you're enjoying the fruits of my labor." She chuckled at her own pun.

Leaning back, he braced his arms on the step behind him and stretched out his legs, drawing her gaze to his long, lean body. She absently licked her bottom lip as she took in his naked chest, the sprinkling of dark hair on his flat, sinewy belly that disappeared into the waistband of his worn jeans, and the heavy bulge beneath the zippered fly. Fantasies danced in her head, of straddling his hips and having her wicked way with him right here on the front porch.

"So, did you find everything you were looking for in Atlanta?" he asked, startling her out of her wayward thoughts.

She focused on his face and found him regarding her seriously. He was honestly interested about her life in Atlanta, but how did she explain that she'd found only what she believed would make her grandmother proud of her, but in the process she'd lost herself and everything that truly mattered to her. She'd compromised what her heart desired and her own personal values to fulfill an old woman's dream of seeing Tess prevail where her own daughter had gone astray.

She looked away from him. "No," she said, her voice near a whisper and her chest tight with all those old regrets. "I can't say I did find what I was looking for." Not when all she ever wanted had been right here in Wynhaven.

"Before your grandmother passed away, there was a rumor that you'd gotten engaged to a lawyer."

Her stomach pitched, and she squeezed her eyes shut, hating the thread of censure she heard in his tone. When she opened them again moments later, she forced herself to look Morgan in the eye and be truthful with him. "It wasn't a rumor. I *was* engaged. As in past tense."

"What happened?" he asked gruffly.

She shrugged, striving for nonchalance, though she felt anything but. "I met Patrick O'Neal at a work function. He was a young, up-and-coming lawyer who worked for his father's firm and we hit it off pretty well. One thing led to another, and before I knew it he was proposing to me, even before I'd met his parents. It all happened so quickly, and I guess I was just caught up in the moment." And though the engagement didn't feel right in her heart, in the back of her mind she kept telling herself this is what her grandmother had been hoping for her. That Helen would be thrilled that her granddaughter had achieved so much and managed to land herself a prominent man to marry.

But marrying Patrick wasn't at all what *Tess* had

wanted, not when so much of what was in her heart still belonged to Morgan. She'd been torn and confused . . . until that fateful night when she'd met his parents, Owen and Ginger O'Neal, and she'd realized what a huge mistake she'd made in accepting Patrick's proposal.

Patrick had taken her to his parents for dinner, introduced her as his fiancée, and it was evident that his mother hadn't been happy about her son's unexpected engagement to a woman they didn't even know. Ginger had no qualms about grilling Tess over their five course meal about her family, her past, and where she'd grown up. As the conversation progressed and Ginger learned that Tess didn't know who her father was, that her mother passed away when she was eight, and that her grandmother did her best to raise her on her own, it became increasingly obvious that Mrs. O'Neal completely disapproved of her. That Tess's lack of any social standing didn't fit into her plans for her son.

The whole evening had been upsetting to Tess on a variety of levels. She'd excused herself to use the bathroom to calm her churning stomach, but she hadn't been able to shake the growing doubts about her marriage to Patrick. On her way back to the living room, she overheard Ginger telling Patrick that Tess was white trash, that she was the kind of woman he should sleep with and get out of his system, and not the kind of girl they expected him to marry.

While Ginger's comment had stunned her, it had been the impetus that Tess had needed to break things off with Patrick, which she'd done that evening when he'd taken her home. And as she lay in bed that night she'd come to realize just how hurt Morgan must have been over her own grandmother's disapproval of him—just as she'd experienced with Ginger O'Neal. Tess hated that he, too, had been the recipient of that kind of pain.

Helen hadn't thought Morgan was good enough for Tess, that as a handyman he didn't have anything significant to offer her. And at the age of eighteen, Tess had been too young and impressionable when it came to pleasing her grandmother, even at the cost of her own desires and emotions.

"Why did you break up with the guy?" Morgan asked, interrupting her private thoughts.

She swallowed hard and managed a halfhearted smile. "Bottom line, I wasn't in love with Patrick, and I got engaged to him for all the wrong reasons. I was just lucky I realized it in time."

Morgan nodded, though he didn't care for what he'd just heard. Still, eight years was a long time to be apart, and they'd both lived separate lives and he supposed they'd each made choices that they now regretted—such as the slew of women he'd used to try and forget about Tess, which had only cemented the truth he'd fought valiantly to ignore. That there was no erasing *this* woman from his soul.

It was difficult for him to imagine her being engaged to another man when she'd been *his,* but he appreciated her honesty, which was something she'd given him this past week, as well as glimpses of the strong, independent woman she'd become. And as a result, he was coming to realize that he still felt something for Tess Monroe. That beyond the pain of losing her, all those emotions he'd buried after her departure eight years ago were gradually finding their way back to the surface.

This wasn't a good thing. Not at all, he thought with a frown. Whatever was between him and Tess now was supposed to be all about seducing her, and nothing about falling hard for her all over again. She was a brief summer fling, nothing more, and he'd do well to remember that since she had no intention of sticking around once the house was repaired and sold.

With that thought firmly embedded in his mind, he abruptly stood. "I better get back to work so I can get this porch finished before the sun sets."

"Okay." She stared at him curiously, obviously a bit perplexed by his sudden shift in mood. Slowly, she stood, too, and gathered up the empty plate and tumbler. "I guess I'll go and pack up a care package for you to take home."

Morgan watched her go, and exhaled a harsh breath. Without a doubt, the woman was turning him inside out—emotionally and physically. And because he refused to succumb to his feelings for her once again, it was time to turn up the heat between them and start the process of getting her out of his system, once and for all.

CHAPTER ◆ FOUR

Morgan returned the following day to finish up the work on the railing around the porch. It only took him a few hours to get the piece work and trim done, and by noon he'd completed the task. Which left him the rest of Saturday afternoon to focus on Tess, and *them*.

He entered the house through the front door in search of Tess and called her name. When he didn't get an answer, he headed into the vacant kitchen. It wasn't until he glanced out the window over the sink that he finally found her out in the backyard, picking a new batch of ripe peaches.

Removing his tool belt, he washed up his hands and arms with soap and water as he watched Tess outside. He grinned as she stood on her tiptoes to pluck the fruit from its stem, which caused her denim mini-skirt to rise a few inches up her thighs. When she turned around, his gaze took in those full breasts beneath her T-shirt, and his groin stirred in instantaneous awareness.

Oh, yeah, they were so done with flirting and teasing, he decided as he dried his hands with a paper towel. Done with all the verbal foreplay and the arousing kisses that had them both aching for more. He wanted Tess, and they were about to give in to what he knew they both had been craving for the past week and a half. They were all alone for the afternoon, and he planned to take full advantage of that fact.

Five minutes later, she entered the kitchen with a bowl filled with peaches. She blew out an upward stream of breath that ruffled her bangs and dumped the fruit into the colander in the sink.

"I can't believe how many peaches those trees produce," she grumbled with a shake of her head. "I can't keep up with it all, and I'm running out of recipes to make. I've tried everything from peach ice cream, to muffins, to custard, and anything else you can imagine. I think I'm finally tapped out of recipes."

He picked up one of the peaches, and feeling how soft and ripe it was beneath his kneading fingers, an idea formed in his mind. One that promised to be fun and sexy and oh-so-erotic.

His blood hummed with anticipation, and he slanted her a sidelong glance. "I sure would hate to see these ripe peaches go to waste."

A frown wrinkled her forehead and she propped her hands on her hips as she considered the fate of the fruit. It was clear that she was lost in her own thoughts and had no clue that he was about to seduce that T-shirt and skirt right off her body.

"Me, too," she said, meeting his gaze with a sigh. "But I'm beginning to feel that if I look at another peach I'm going to turn into one."

Which didn't sound like a bad thing to Morgan, not when he knew how sweet and juicy she'd taste. "I think I need to give you a new appreciation for peaches," he drawled with shameless intent, and slowly backed her up against the counter as he continued to palm the fruit in his hand. "Something to inspire you for later, when you're trying to come up with a new recipe for all those peaches."

Her eyes widened as she finally realized what he was up to. "Why Morgan, are you trying to get into my pants?"

He laughed, enjoying her playful humor. "I believe I am, Ms. Monroe. Is it working?"

Her eyes smoldered with come-hither desire. "Not yet, but I'm more than willing to let you give it your best shot."

Permission granted, he put his seductive plan into motion. He lifted the peach to her mouth and rubbed the fuzzy skin against her bottom lip. "Take a bite," he murmured.

Obeying his order, her lips parted and her teeth sank into the fruit at the same time that Morgan squeezed, causing the juice to dribble down her chin. She gasped in surprise, and when she automatically lifted her hand to catch the juice before it made a mess on her T-shirt, he caught her wrist and held her off. He took a bite of the fruit, too, then went in for a deep, tongue-tangling, peach-flavored kiss. The taste of her was hot and intoxicating and incredibly sweet, and he was dying to sample her elsewhere.

Between kisses, he skimmed her shirt up and off, then deftly removed her bra and let it fall to the floor without so much as a hint of a protest from her. With his mouth still fused to hers, he mashed up another peach over the sink, pushed the pit out with his thumb, and proceeded to slather her chest with the cool pulp.

She sucked in a quick breath and pulled her mouth from his, her expression filled with shocked disbelief at his actions. "What are you doing?"

He shaped her lovely breasts in his palms and grazed his thumbs over her hard, tight nipples, all but devouring her gorgeous body with his gaze. "I'm creating a new peach recipe."

A shiver coursed through her, and her mouth tipped in a sexy smile. "What's it called?" she asked breathlessly.

"Peach ecstasy," he said, and swept his hand downward, painting sticky, slippery swirls over her flat stomach.

Her breathing deepened, and her eyes rolled back when he dipped his finger into her navel—slowly, provocatively, again and again. "It's, umm, very messy to make."

And it was going to get a whole lot messier before he was done. "Don't worry, I have every intention of cleaning up after myself."

He kissed her again as he unsnapped the front of her mini-skirt, then hooked his thumbs inside the waistband and pushed the denim and her silky panties down her legs. They dropped to her feet with a muted thump, and she stepped out of the garments and kicked them aside, along with the sandals she'd been wearing.

The thought of finally having her naked made him harder than he could remember being in a long time. Clasping his strong hands around her waist, he lifted her up so she was sitting on the counter in front of him and on display for his viewing pleasure. He dragged his mouth from hers, took a small step back, and looked his fill of those womanly curves glistening with peach nectar, her long, shapely limbs that had spurred some of his most fondest fantasies, and all that made her completely and utterly feminine.

Warmth suffused Tess's entire body as a bout of self-consciousness settled over her, making her feel much too vulnerable with this man, physically and emotionally. Morgan's eyes were the color of heated liquid silver, his features taut with lust and need as his gaze ravished her as she knew his mouth would eventually do.

She resisted the urge to lift her hands and cover herself. "Morgan . . ." Her voice quivered, as did her nerve-endings.

He continued to stare, his gaze drifting from her breasts down to the thatch of hair between her thighs. "God, you're so beautiful, Tess," he said, his low pitched tone filled with awe and male appreciation. "All of you."

Undeniable pleasure bloomed deep inside of her, but

she still felt so bare compared to him, and told him so. "You're much too overdressed."

He grinned, whipped his shirt over his head, and dropped it to the floor. "Better?"

"For now." She reached out and pressed her hands to his chest, needing that physical connection to him. His skin was hot and firm, and his heart beat heavily beneath her palm, a reassuring rhythm that matched her own. And when she plucked his nipples with her fingers, she was gratified to hear a low growl erupt from the back of his throat.

"Damn, you're distracting me." He caught her wandering hands before they could slide southward, and secured them back to her sides. "Behave. I'm not done with *you* yet."

She bit her bottom lip, mostly to hide a smile. "Sorry," she murmured, but she really wasn't at all contrite for making him a little bit wild, too.

"Now where was I?" He reached for another peach, mashed it up, and turned back to her as he gently urged her legs further apart. "Ahhh, now I remember," he said, and smeared the slick mixture all the way up both of her thighs, until his calloused, peach-coated thumbs grazed the outer lips of her sex, then slid deeper, teasing her with soft, sweeping strokes that made her hot and wet and restless for so much more.

He lifted his gaze from where his fingers were wreaking havoc on her body and senses, and grinned lazily. "I think the recipe is just about done."

Except there was one key ingredient missing. "What happened to the *ecstasy* part?"

"That's gonna happen right now, when I eat you up," he said, an unholy gleam in his eyes.

Lowering his head, he slowly, meticulously licked away the pureed peach glazing her breasts, and used his lips and teeth and tongue to catch every delicious drop. He drew her nipple into the wet warmth of his mouth and swirled his tongue over the tender tip, then pulled her in deeper, suckling on her in a strong, rhythmic motion that had her hands tangling in his thick, silky hair, and a long, low moan erupting from her chest.

He continued his downward descent, his soft, hot tongue lapping and swirling its way to her quivering belly. He spent a frustrating amount of time making sure he removed every bit of nectar and pulp from her navel before he began licking and nibbling his way up one trembling thigh, then the other, until there was only one last treat for him to enjoy.

He pushed her legs wider apart, slid his hands beneath her bottom, and pulled her to the edge of the counter. Her hips automatically tilted upward for him, the position forcing her to brace her hands behind her to support herself.

His dark eyes were centered between her thighs and his nostrils flared as he took in her swollen, wet flesh. She felt the rush of anticipation build so high it made her dizzy. Her entire body pulsed and silently begged for the possession to come, knowing that it wasn't going to take much to make her fly apart for him.

He knew exactly what to do to make that happen. With a raw groan he took her intimately, drawing the sweet peach essence of her into his mouth, feasting on her like a man who'd gone too long without sustenance. She felt his long, work-roughened fingers join in, sliding through her plump folds before he pushed one, then another, deep inside her body. He withdrew them both slowly, thrust them back in just as languidly, making her melt around his fingers. His tongue circled her straining clit, and then he fastened his mouth over her sex and sucked, hard and strong.

The shock of sensation rippled through her, pushing her over that precarious edge between pleasure and the bliss her body longed for. She cried out as her orgasm completely consumed her, the release as much physical as it was emotional.

As promised, he gave her ecstasy in its purest form.

He came back up and kissed her, slowly, thoroughly, while soothing her with the tender caress of his big hands down her bare back until the tremors within her calmed. But there was no mistaking the intensity and need still gripping him, and that knowledge spurred her to lavish him with as much pleasure as he'd just given her.

Deepening the connection of their mouths, she wrapped her arms around his neck. Using him for an anchor, she scooted off the counter and slid her body down the length of his until her feet touched the floor. Her breasts rubbed against his hot, naked chest, smearing the sticky residue of peaches along his flesh. Denim scratched her bare thighs, and his fierce erection pressed insistently against her mound.

It took her less than a minute to free his erect penis from the fly of his jeans and wrap her hand around his thick, straining cock. He pulled his mouth from hers and groaned, even as his hips thrust instinctively against her tight grip in a quest for satisfaction.

Holding Morgan's heavy lidded gaze, she reached for one of the succulent peaches in the sink and proceeded to knead it into a nice pulpy consistency. "Now it's my turn to test out that recipe of yours."

He visibly shuddered. "God, I was hoping you were going to say that."

She laughed huskily and stroked him from base to tip, covering him with the delectable, sumptuous fruit. Then she knelt on the floor in front of Morgan and took him into her mouth. She teased him with her tongue and licked him clean of the sweet peach nectar. His breathing grew ragged and his hips jerked as she sucked him deeper, her lips and fingers and tongue sliding sensuously along his shaft.

"Oh, Christ," he hissed, his voice low and guttural with warning. "I'm going to come."

A large hand came to rest at the back of her head, gently urging her mouth further over him, yet giving her enough slack to pull back if she wished. But she was just as caught up in the moment as he was, the taste and texture of him exciting her, and she took him all the way because she wanted to. Because she'd dreamt and fantasized of this moment for years.

He came on a lustful groan, and when he finally recovered from the shattering intensity of his release she stood back up, gratified to see him looking so dazed and wasted. Especially knowing she'd been the one to do that to him.

She placed her hand on his chest and when her fingers stuck to his skin, she grimaced. She was gooey all over, too, and now that the peach substance was drying, it was becoming increasingly uncomfortable on her skin.

"What a mess we made," she said in amusement, knowing she'd never be able to eat another peach again without thinking of Morgan's erotic recipe. "I think we both need a shower."

He feathered the back of his fingers over the swollen tips of her breasts and stared down at her, a boyish grin curving the corners of his mouth. "Is that an invitation for me to stay?"

Her heart thumped hard in her chest. This encounter in the kitchen had been fun and all about sex and carnal pleasure, but she had a feeling that anything more with Morgan would involve her heart on a very emotional level.

Hell, who was she kidding? Her feelings for him were already tied up into a huge gigantic knot, despite the fact that he wasn't offering her any promises other than the kind that involved physical gratification, and lots of it.

Still, knowing that, she did her best to accept their affair for what it was, determined to enjoy her time with Morgan for as long as it lasted.

Clasping his hand in hers, she smiled. "Yeah, it is an invitation."

She led him upstairs, and minutes later they were in a hot, steamy shower together, washing away the pulp and nectar from their skin. They shared slow, soft, open-mouthed kisses while caressing and stroking slick flesh with their hands and fingers, and took their time exploring each other's bodies and relearning all those sweet, hot spots that turned them on the most. And there were plenty of them to rediscover.

The foreplay was exquisite, the gradual build up to another desperate hunger just as keen, arousing them both all over again. Desire and need and soft moans of pleasure swirled around them, mingling with the steam and warm spray of water, intensifying every provocative touch until the water turned cool and finally forced them out of the shower.

They dried off and made their way into Tess's bedroom. Once there, Morgan pushed her back on the bed and came up and over her, positioning himself between her already spread thighs. He stared down at her face, his dark hair damp and tousled around his head, his features taut with restraint, and his hard, strong body a direct contrast to how soft and warm and pliant hers was beneath his.

Then he closed his eyes and cursed beneath his

breath. "Please tell me you're on the Pill or have a condom handy."

If she wasn't strung so tight, she would have laughed. Instead, she was eternally grateful that she'd remained on the contraceptive after breaking up with Patrick. "I'm on the Pill."

His sigh of relief shuddered through his entire body, and he finally pushed slowly inside her. He filled her inch by exquisite inch, stretching her to accommodate his size and length until he was finally buried to the hilt. Then he dropped his head against the curve of her neck, and his long groan of satisfaction was matched by her own.

"You feel so damn good," he muttered, his breath blowing hot and damp against her skin.

She slid her hands down the arch of his spine to his buttocks, and turned her face toward his, letting her lips drift across his cheek. "So do you," she whispered, and wrapped her legs around the back of his thighs, urging him to *move,* to take her hard and fast and mindlessly deep.

He seemed to need that as well, and began to thrust into her, high and hard, stealing her breath with the sudden force of his passion for her. He rolled his hips, grinding against her sex, stroking deeper, then deeper still, until she had no idea where he ended and she began.

Abruptly, he lifted up on his forearms. He framed her face in his hands and watched her changing expression as he drove into her again, pushing her closer and closer to that white-hot release beckoning just beyond her reach. His hips pumped relentlessly, his gaze fierce on hers, and she knew he was waiting for her climax to peak before he allowed himself to succumb to his own.

"Come on, baby, it's right *there,*" he urged desperately. "I can *feel* it."

Yes, she could feel it, too. Despite the years that had separated them, it amazed her that he still knew her body so well, and in the next instant her orgasm shuddered through her and her inner muscles clenched violently around his shaft. Her lips parted, but before she could scream he sealed his mouth over hers and kissed her hungrily, possessing her as his and making them one in every way. He growled against her lips as he came right along with her.

When it was over, she was left drained and shaking and awed by the sheer power this one man still had over her—body and soul.

After spending the rest of the afternoon wallowing in complete and utter sexual satisfaction, Morgan finally let Tess give into her physical exhaustion and drift off to sleep. He lay on his side facing her, content to watch her as she napped, thinking he'd never seen her look so serene and beautiful.

Her blond hair was a disheveled mess from his hands and fingers that had tangled in the silken strands during the throes of one of their many trysts, her mouth was swollen from all their deep, lush kisses, and her skin was flushed a becoming shade of pink that looked incredibly good on her.

That easily, his body stirred once again, wanting her, despite how many times and the different ways he'd just taken her. After they'd recovered from the first round, he'd turned her over onto her stomach and made love to her again in what had always been their favorite position—with Tess on her hands and knees, his cock buried into her from behind, and him in complete control of her pleasure.

Now older and more appreciative of Tess's body and all the secret wonders it had to offer, he decided he liked it best when she was on top of him, straddling his hips and riding his body like she owned him while he caressed her full breasts, her sensitive belly, and that oh-so-responsive flesh between her smooth, slender thighs.

Sex between them had always been good, but this time it had been mind-blowing and stunning in its intensity. Certainly there had been lust and desire and passion, which were all the ingredients that made for a hell of a good lay.

But what Morgan hadn't expected was the shift he'd felt in his emotions that made it excruciating clear that he was still in love with Tess Monroe. That beneath the resentment and pain of her leaving him all those years ago, he knew there would never be another woman who completed him the way she did. And there would never be another woman who had the ability to make him long for the kind of things he'd always wanted with Tess: love, marriage, family.

Despite what had happened in the past, he could no longer deny that those three things were intrinsically linked to her, and he knew they always would be. And he was so damn tired of fighting his feelings for her.

The truth hit him hard, and he rolled to his back and closed his eyes, wondering if maybe things could be different this time around. They'd both matured and were older and wiser about many things, but was it possible for the two of them to find their way back to each other after all that had passed between them? And could he convince her to stay in Wynhaven when she was so intent on selling her grandmother's house—her final tie to the town she'd grown up in—and when she still had a life waiting for her in Atlanta?

Unfortunately, there were no easy answers for his questions, and he knew any choice Tess made about him or her future would have to be hers and hers alone. He wasn't going to beg her to stay, but for the duration of her time in Wynhaven he could show her what could be, if she was at all interested in what he had to offer. Worse case, they'd part ways at the end of their affair as friends, which was more than they'd had for the past eight years. Not that that would ever be enough for him when it came to Tess.

His stomach rumbled hungrily, bringing him out of his thoughts and reminding him that he'd skipped lunch. He grinned wryly. A man couldn't live on peaches alone, not even when eaten straight off of Tess's luscious body. He needed food, a real meal, and he knew Tess would be hungry when she awoke, too.

He slid out of bed, put his jeans on, and padded down to the kitchen to put something together for the two of them. He cleaned up the peach mess they'd made, then found the makings for ham and cheese sandwiches, and he piled his twice as thick with the meat. He set the sandwiches on two separate paper plates, along with spoonfuls of the potato salad she'd bought at the deli, then poured two glasses of iced tea.

He turned to go wake up Tess, and came to an abrupt stop when he found her standing in the doorway, silently watching him with one of those soft smiles on her lips. She was wearing a pair of light drawstring sweats and an oversized T-shirt, which hid those tempting curves he'd just spent hours enjoying.

"I was just coming to get you. Hungry?" he asked, and carried their plates to the table before coming back for their drinks.

"Ummm, I'm starved." She took the seat next to his and took a bite of the potato salad. "You made me work up an appetite this afternoon."

"Well, eat up, sweetheart, because we still have the whole night ahead of us," he teased. He waggled his brows at her, and started in on his sandwich.

She groaned, but there was laughter in her eyes. "You're insatiable."

"Not once did I hear the words 'I've had enough' come from those pretty lips of yours."

She ducked her head, but not before he caught the flush of pink spreading across her cheekbones. "You're shameless, too, you know that?"

He chuckled, enjoying their banter. Enjoying her. "It's all a part of my Southern charm," he drawled.

They ate their sandwiches and talked about his schedule for the upcoming week and what he had planned. His focus would be on the inside of the house, starting with the kitchen floor, cabinets, and counter-tops. Another week or two and the biggest part of the renovations would be done, he told her.

"Will you be here tomorrow?" she asked.

It was Sunday, a day he usually reserved all to him-self. He normally spent the morning and afternoon working on the pieces of oak furniture he sold on con-signment. "I wasn't planning on it."

She nodded in understanding and glanced away, and he realized she'd most likely spend tomorrow all by her-self in this big old house. Suddenly he didn't want even a day to go by without being with her. Especially since he didn't know how much time they had left to spend together.

Finished with his meal, he pushed his empty plate aside. "I was thinking . . . since you haven't had the chance to get over to see my sister yet, would you like to go with me to her place for dinner tomorrow evening?"

He saw a flash of delight spark in her eyes before it was quickly doused with uncertainties. "I don't want to intrude on a family dinner."

"I wouldn't extend the invitation if I knew you wouldn't be welcome, Tess." He reached out and ten-derly traced the line of her jaw with his finger. He wanted this for her, a reconciliation between the two women who'd been such close childhood friends. "Say *yes,* sweetheart," he cajoled in a deep, inviting tone.

A slow, tentative smile appeared on her lips, chasing away the doubts he'd seen in her gaze. "All right. I'd love to go with you."

"Great. I'll let Amy know." He kissed her on the cheek and stood, clearing their paper plates and tossing them into the trash. "I guess I should head home."

She set their empty glasses into the sink and cast him a sidelong glance that did little to disguise her disappointment. "What about the night that's still ahead of us?"

He slid his arms around her waist and pulled her flush to his body. "I could spend the next two days making love to you, but I don't want to wear out my welcome and you should get some rest."

"I'm fine," she assured him, then placed her hands on his chest and bit her bottom lip. "How about we relax together?" she suggested instead. "I picked up a few DVDs at the rental place when I was out this morning. Would you like to watch a movie with me tonight? I'd love to have the company."

The hopeful note he heard in her voice grabbed at him, making it difficult for him to refuse her simple request. She obviously didn't want to be alone, and he didn't want to leave, either.

"Are you going to make me suffer though a chick flick?" he grumbled good-naturedly.

Her eyes opened wide in feigned innocence. "Would you? For me?"

He released a long-suffering sigh, like any self-respecting male would expect him to do. "If you insist."

Pleased with his acquiescence, she laughed and led him merrily to the living room, where she proceeded to set up the DVD, then cuddled up next to him on the couch. Even as he settled in to watch *Sweet Home Alabama* with Tess, a movie he'd never had any interest in seeing because of its romantic, sentimental content, he was coming to realize and accept that he'd do just about anything this woman asked of him.

Anything at all.

CHAPTER ◆ FIVE

Tess's stomach fluttered anxiously as Morgan brought his truck to a stop in front of his sister's place. She couldn't help but be a little nervous about seeing Amy for the first time in so many years, no matter how much Morgan had tried to reassure her that his sister was thrilled that she was coming for dinner today.

She glanced at the house that Amy now lived in with her husband and kids, a small but well-maintained single story structure with an abundance of green plants and vibrant roses growing in the flower beds leading up to the front porch. A Big Wheel was parked haphazardly in the middle of the driveway, along with a scooter; evidence of the two little boys who lived there and who were currently kicking a soccer ball across the front yard to each other.

As soon as they saw Morgan, their faces lit up and

they raced across the lawn chorusing in excitement, "Uncle Morgan, Uncle Morgan!"

They greeted him as soon as he stepped out of the truck, and Morgan hefted them both into his arms at the same time. He made a deep growling sound, pretending to be a big, ferocious bear who'd captured them.

Both boys squirmed in his strong arms and squealed with delight, obviously reveling in their uncle's attention and playful side. Tess slid from the truck with the basket of goodies she'd brought for the Barber family and found herself smiling and enjoying the moment, too.

Morgan set the boys back down on the sidewalk, and the one who looked the oldest of the pair peered up at Tess with avid interest. "Who's the lady, Uncle Morgan?"

Morgan ruffled the boy's dark brown hair affectionately. "This is my friend, Tess Monroe."

"Hello," Tess said, and recalled the names that Morgan had given her for the six- and four-year-old. "Let's see . . . you must be Todd." At the boy's nod, she glanced at the other youngster, who was standing at Morgan's side, not quite as outgoing as his older brother. "And you must be Gavin."

"That's right," Todd said, sounding surprised at her knowledge. "Do you know us?"

"Your uncle told me who you are," Tess said with a smile, seeing a bit of Amy's resemblance in Todd's young, animated face. "But I do know your mom, and your dad, too. We all went to school together." Jake Barber had always had a crush on Amy, and Tess was thrilled that the two of them had ended up happily married.

"What's in the basket?" Gavin asked in a quiet little voice, his curiosity getting the best of him, despite his attempt at being shy and clinging to his Uncle's leg.

"I brought some peach jam for your mom and dad," she said, and almost laughed when Todd made an "ick" kind of face and dramatically shuddered. "And I also made chocolate chip cookies." She didn't think that a four- and six-year-old would have appreciated a peach muffin or turnover.

She lifted the cloth covering the baked goods, and the rich, redolent scent of fresh homemade cookies wafted right below the little boys' noses. "Would you each like one?"

Wide-eyed and hopeful, both youngsters glanced up at Morgan for his approval. "Can we, Uncle Morgan?" Todd asked.

"Go ahead," he said with a nod. "I'm sure your mom won't mind you having one cookie before dinner."

The two boys crowded around the basket and took the biggest cookie each one of them could find, and the treat was all it took for Tess to win both of the boys over.

Once Todd and Gavin were busy eating their cookies, Morgan tucked Tess's free hand in his and walked with her up to the front porch. As they neared the house, those nervous butterflies in Tess's belly rehatched. She hoped that Amy was just as quick to accept her into her life as the boys had just been.

As they entered the house and Amy came into the living room to greet her and Morgan, Tess realized that her fears were completely unfounded. Amy, with her big pregnant belly, didn't hesitate to wrap Tess in a warm hug as soon as they saw one another. Tess returned the embrace just as wholeheartedly, the years between them melting away as if they'd never been apart.

Finally, Amy let her go and stepped back, her gaze taking in Tess's appearance. "God, you look so gorgeous and sophisticated. I feel so frumpy in comparison!" She indicated her own maternity dress in comparison to Tess's cute summer top and flowing cotton skirt.

"You look radiant, Amy," Tess said, and meant it. "Obviously being pregnant agrees with you because you absolutely glow."

Amy's husband, Jake, greeted Tess with a light kiss on her cheek, then slipped his arms around his wife's waist from behind and rubbed her burgeoning belly. "I keep telling her she's the most beautiful woman I know."

Amy rolled her eyes, though it was evident by the undisguised fondness in her gaze that she adored her husband. "You're my husband. You're supposed to think I'm a goddess no matter what."

They all laughed and followed Amy into the kitchen, where she'd been preparing dinner. Amy handed each of the men a cold bottle of beer and sent them out back to fire up the barbeque while she finished getting the chicken ready to put on the grill. Tess offered to help, and Amy gave her the task of making the salad.

They immediately fell into easy conversation, without a trace of awkwardness between them as they spent the next forty minutes trying to catch up on each other's lives. Tess added cut-up tomatoes to the bowl of lettuce while telling Amy about Atlanta. Her old friend filled her in on all the latest gossip in Wynhaven, as well as what had been going on in her own personal life with Jake and the boys, including the new baby on the way, which was due in less than two months. Tess experienced a small pinch of envy for all that Amy had gained over the years. Unconditional love. A great husband. A wonderful family.

Tess felt as though her college degree, small apartment, and currently unemployed status paled in comparison.

Dinner was a lively affair, with Todd and Gavin doing their best to entertain their Uncle Morgan and his guest with silly antics that had Tess covering her laughter behind her napkin so she didn't laugh out loud and encourage the two imps. Amy was certain that Morgan was somehow egging the two boys on, and though her brother swore he was an innocent bystander, Tess had to agree with Amy since she recognized that mischievous gleam in Morgan's gaze as he glanced at Todd and Gavin and the two boys burst into fits of giggles all over again.

Once the meal was over, Tess helped Amy clear the table, put away the leftovers, and clean up the kitchen. Then with a plate of her chocolate chip cookies in hand, they joined the men out in the backyard, who were playing ball with the boys and taking advantage of the last bit of sunlight.

Tess settled next to Amy on the porch swing, and they set it into motion with easy pushes of their feet. Quiet moments passed as they watched the men and boys having fun, and finally Amy glanced Tess's way and broke the silence between them.

"So, what's going on between you and Morgan?" Amy asked.

On some level Tess had expected the question, so it didn't come as a surprise. But she wasn't about to share the intimate details of her current relationship with Morgan with his sister, so she opted for the business version.

Tess met her friend's curious gaze and smiled. "I'm sure Morgan told you I hired him to renovate my grandmother's house before I put it up for sale."

Amy rested a hand on her belly and lifted a skeptical brow. "So you both say."

There was no mistaking the blatant disbelief in Amy's tone, but Tess refused to give anything away. "What's that supposed to mean? It's the truth."

"Honestly, it's none of my business what's really going on between the two of you, but it's obvious that it's more than a working relationship."

Tess wondered how she'd come to that conclusion, since Tess had been very careful about keeping things between her and Morgan low key in front of his sister and her family. Somehow, Amy had seen through the ruse.

Amy waited for her to reply, but when Tess remained quiet, neither confirming or denying the claim, Amy went on.

"Morgan was so hurt when you broke things off with him and left for Atlanta," Amy said, her gaze drifting back to the man they were discussing. "And it took him a long time to get over you, if he ever did."

Tess felt a lump of emotion rise in her throat, because if she'd learned anything at all since returning to Wynhaven, it was that she'd never, ever, gotten over Morgan either. To think he felt the same shook her up inside.

"I've been watching the fascinated way he looks at you, Tess, and he's definitely falling for you all over again," Amy continued softly. "I haven't seen him look at another woman like that since you."

Tess shivered as Amy's profound statement stole through her. Was it possible that Morgan might want her for more than just a passing fancy? Her heart and emotions wanted to believe it could be true, but her practical side reminded her that though she was sleeping with Morgan, he'd given her no guarantees other than a good time. And her own life was still so undecided that she wasn't in the position to make promises to him, either.

Amy reached over and touched Tess's hand, prompting Tess to meet her friend's gaze once again. "I know Morgan is an adult and he can make his own decisions, but I don't want him to get hurt again when you leave." The sisterly concern in her voice was evident.

The last thing Tess wanted was to cause Morgan any more pain, but she'd like to believe that this time between her and Morgan was different than before. Because even if her decision took her back to Atlanta, she and Morgan had at least forged a new friendship that would hopefully sustain more than just her brief visit in Wynhaven.

Before she could formulate a response, the boys and men joined them on the porch, effectively dispelling Tess and Amy's private conversation. Everyone helped themselves to the cookies, and after a half hour of more amusing antics from Todd and Gavin that kept the adults entertained, Amy stood up and pressed a hand to her aching back.

"Okay, boys, that's enough of your silliness," Amy chided gently. "Time for your baths."

"Aww, Mom, do we have to?" Todd complained with a pout. "Uncle Morgan and Tess are still here."

"Actually, it's getting late and we should get going," Morgan said. Clasping Tess's hand securely in his, he helped her up from the swing.

Tess thanked Jake and Amy for having her over for dinner, and said good-bye to the boys. Todd gave her a big hug and told her she made the best chocolate chip cookies ever. Four-year-old Gavin approached her more timidly and looked up at her with big brown eyes.

"Will you come over again with Uncle Morgan?" Gavin asked.

The bright anticipation in his gaze told Tess that this little boy had come to accept her, and she was touched that he wanted to see her again. But since her time in Wynhaven was still so unsettled, she kept her reply as noncommittal as possible.

"I hope so," she said with a smile, and that seemed to satisfy the little boy.

She and Morgan left the Barber's and ten minutes later they were pulling into a long, graveled driveway that led to a beautiful, sprawling house tucked away from anyone who drove along the main street.

She glanced back at him in surprise. "Is this your place?" she asked.

"Yep." He grinned, the pride on his face unmistakable. "I bought the property about three years ago and built the house on it."

What she found most ironic was the fact that Morgan's property bordered against her grandmother's, with only a quarter mile of green, lush forest separating them. And he'd never told her.

She shook her head in amazement, and though she was glad he'd brought her to his place, she wasn't sure what had prompted him to do so now. Bringing her to where he lived seemed so intimate, so personal, and way beyond what their affair had been about so far.

The subtle shift in their relationship threw her off-kilter, prompting her to ask the question that was running through her head. "What are we doing here?"

His gaze met hers with a warmth and tenderness that made her heart leap in her chest. "There's something I want to share with you."

His choice of words added to her curiosity, and when they walked into his house hand in hand minutes later and she saw all the oak furniture filling his home she instinctively knew that he'd hand-crafted the end tables, coat-rack, and wall-unit in the living room, as well as the table, chairs, and china hutch in the dining room.

"You made all this, didn't you?" she asked, indicating everything with a sweep of her hand.

He nodded. "Yes, I did."

"Oh, Morgan," she breathed in pure appreciation of his talent. All the pieces were beautiful, unique, and exquisitely designed, a real testament to just how brilliant this man was with his hands and mind.

She trailed her fingers over the polished surface of the large dining room table, admiring the smooth scalloped edges and the way the chairs matched exactly. "Why don't you sell the furniture you make? You'd make a mint on custom orders."

"I do." He pushed his hands into the front pockets of his jeans, and she could tell he was trying to be modest about his hand-crafted furniture. "All those pieces you saw in my workshop behind my office, those are ordered pieces, and ones I sell on consignment in a few places. I've got the construction as my main source of income, but the furniture I make in my spare time brings in a good amount of money, too, and it's something I enjoy."

The man was certainly full of surprises, and she grinned at him, happy for his own personal success. "I suppose I should put my order in now for a Morgan Kane original, before high demand drives up your prices."

He laughed, the deep, rich sound curling seductively through her. "I think I can cut you a break." He winked at her and led her down a long hallway. "Come on, what I want to share with you is this way."

They passed a few bedrooms, and Tess caught a brief glimpse of a guest room, a home office, and a work-out room, until finally they walked into a large, spacious master bedroom decorated in beige and hunter green tones. More of Morgan's woodwork furnished the room, but it was the king-sized four poster bed that caught her attention. Like everything else he'd made, it was beautiful and elegantly detailed, a one of a kind piece that complemented the armoire across from it.

She turned back around and cast Morgan a sly, teasing look. "Was this just a ploy to get me into your bedroom?"

Morgan chuckled. "I don't think I need a ploy for that." He moved to the other side of the room, to where he'd put the special gift he'd made for Tess so many years ago, but had never had the chance to give her. "Actually, what I want to show you is right here."

She came up to where he was standing, and he met her gaze, suddenly feeling oddly vulnerable, because of what this gift was going to reveal. It was time to make peace with the past, and this was his way of showing Tess how much she still meant to him without scaring her off with a declaration of love before she was ready to hear those words.

"It's a hope chest," she said softly, and knelt before the chest to get a better look at it. "A beautiful one."

"I was hoping you'd think so." He watched her open the box to see the inside and he inhaled the scent of cedar, which he'd used to line the interior of the chest. "I made it for you years ago, when we were dating."

She glanced up at him, her eyes wide and startled, and a bit confused, too. "You did?"

He nodded. "I didn't get the chance to give it to you before you left for Atlanta, but I want you to have it now."

No matter how upset he'd been with Tess for leaving, he hadn't been able to give away the hope chest, not when there were so many sentimental emotions attached to the piece. Not when she'd been his first and only love.

Besides, it had been personalized just for her.

With her still staring at him in disbelief, he squatted next to her and pointed to the heart and initials he'd carved on top of the box. "See, there's a T and an M right there."

The letters could have stood for Tess Monroe, or Tess and Morgan, and he decided to let her come to her own conclusions about that. Though when he'd whittled that heart and those initials into the wood it had been for the two of them, with the intent that they would be together forever.

He heard a strangled sound come from Tess and she abruptly stood. Unsure what had set her off, he straightened, too, and when he saw the tears filling her eyes and trickling down her cheek, his gut clenched hard.

"Hey, what's this?" he asked gently, and brushed away a fresh tear with his thumb. "I give you a gift and you're crying?"

A smile wavered on her lips, but he could still see how torn and confused she was. "No one has ever given me anything as beautiful or thoughtful as this hope chest. Thank you. I'll treasure it always." She wrapped her arms around his neck and kissed him, softly at first, then with a growing need that quickly flared out of control.

He tasted the escalating desire and passion in the way her mouth melded to his, could sense the emotion in the way her hands touched him, and he knew where all this kissing and caressing was heading. And because he suspected that she wasn't ready to deal with what his gift implied, he willingly gave himself over to the moment, determined to give her the kind of hot, mindless joining she craved, just as much as he did.

He wanted to claim and possess her in the most elemental way possible. Wanted to make sure she knew she was *his* and always would be. With that in mind, he backed her up three steps, until he had her pressed up against the wall with his body. He was already hard, and when he slipped his hand beneath her skirt and pulled off her panties, he found her hot and wet and already ready for him.

With his mouth still on Tess's and her body arching eagerly into his, he cupped her sex, slid his fingers through her soft, slick flesh, and brought her to the brink in only a few provocative strokes.

She pulled her lips from his, and her head rolled back against the wall as she gripped his forearms for support. "Oh, Lord, Morgan," she panted breathlessly. "The bed is right over there."

He ripped open the front placket of his jeans and released his aching erection. He wasn't about to shatter this sensual moment by switching gears now, and he didn't want to give her time to think. All he wanted was for her to just *feel* how he cared about her, and how in love with her he still was. And just how good they were together.

"The bed is too damn far away, and I've spent the entire day thinking about making love to you again," he said as he slid his hands over her curvy bottom and down the back of her thighs. He lifted her against him, spreading her legs so that they gripped his waist and his shaft was poised right at her very core. "I can't wait a second longer to get inside of you."

She laughed throatily, then closed her eyes and moaned as he entered her in one long, smooth thrust. With strong fingers he clutched her hips, working her body exactly the way he wanted, the way they both needed. He drove into her faster, higher, harder, and she met him stroke for stroke, until he finally felt her tumbling over the edge. Her inner muscles pulsed, squeezing him as tight as a fist, beckoning him to follow her straight into that vortex of white-hot pleasure and carnal bliss.

He did exactly that, joining her in that place where nothing existed but him and her, and the incredible rush of losing himself in everything sweet and giving that was Tess Monroe.

CHAPTER ◆ SIX

Tess chewed on her bottom lip as she sat in the town's only real-estate office and listened to Marsha Lawson go on about property values, comps, and how the market was in an upswing and a prime time for sellers. She'd been very excited to see Tess, and even more thrilled to hear that she was planning on putting her grandmother's house up for sale. Tess wasn't sure if the other woman's eagerness had to do with the commission she'd make, or something else that Tess was missing.

After three weeks of hard, intensive labor on Morgan's part, along with occasional help from his crew on the more difficult and time-consuming repairs, the renovations were nearly completed. The new counters in the kitchen had been installed, the cabinets had been resurfaced, and the old linoleum had been ripped up. The hardwood floors beneath had been refinished to a gleaming shine, giving the kitchen a richness and warmth it had previously lacked, and Tess had to admit it was now one of her favorite rooms in the house.

Light fixtures, plumbing, and electrical problems had been repaired. A new oak banister had been installed, and a fresh coat of paint made the once dingy, yellowing walls more appealing and chased away the gloom that had seemed to weigh down the appearance of the house.

What was once a run-down, neglected house now resembled the custom built home it once was, one that looked well-cared for and loved. And now Tess was about to turn her back on the one thing that had given her a sense of stability and security growing up.

She pushed that melancholy thought out of her head. Putting the house on the market was the logical thing to do, or so Tess had been trying to convince herself for the past week and a half. There were only a few minor repairs left to be done, and there was absolutely no way Tess could afford to keep the place. Not when she was unemployed and there wasn't much in the way of finding a decent paying job in Wynhaven. She might have received a nice severance from her previous employer, but that money would only go so far in maintaining a place as big as her grandmother's.

Besides, the house was just too enormous for one person. And much too quiet and lonely, with only herself inhabiting the place.

"I've seen the work that Morgan has been doing out at your grandmother's place," Marsha went on enthusiastically. "And if the inside looks as good as the outside, it shouldn't take me long to find a buyer."

That should have been good news to Tess's ears, but instead it increased the confusion and doubts swirling within her. "Do you know of someone looking for a house in Wynhaven?"

Marsha scribbled a note in Tess's file and glanced back up at her with a bright smile. "No, not specifically, but I have some contacts in Atlanta, and I think that house would make a terrific bed and breakfast. I've always thought so. It's right on the lake, there's plenty of bedrooms and bathrooms, and since the nearest hotel is over twenty miles away, it would be a cozy place for guests to stay if they're passing through Wynhaven or visiting."

Now Tess understood where a good deal of Marsha's eagerness was stemming from. She'd obviously had her eye on Tess's grandmother's place for some time now, with her own plans for the house and property, if she could entice the right buyer. Which Marsha didn't think she'd have a hard time finding at all.

Neither did Tess. She couldn't deny that Marsha's idea was an appealing one. Wynhaven could certainly benefit from a bed and breakfast, but the longer she sat in Marsha's office and listened to the other woman go on about Tess's grandmother's house and all its attributes, Tess became increasingly upset. She didn't like the thought of a stranger transforming the house she'd grown up in, and she realized what a difficult time she was having letting go of the one thing that had been a constant in her life: her grandmother and the only real home she'd ever known.

"I'll get the house and property appraised in the next week and we can get the house on the market." Marsha said, interrupting Tess's thoughts with business details. "I'm sure you're anxious to sell the place so you can return to Atlanta, and I'm certain someone will snap it up in no time at all."

Marsha's secretary buzzed in on the intercom to let her know she had another client waiting, signaling the end to their meeting. After reassuring that she'd be in touch, Tess left the woman's office and returned to her grandmother's house.

There was no one working there today, which Tess had expected since Morgan had been called out to help his guys on a construction project they were having problems on. Morgan had promised her he'd finish up the minor repairs still left to be done in the evenings, after his construction work during the day.

Tess walked into the large, quiet house, and immediately missed having Morgan there. His deep, smooth voice. His sexy, lazy smiles. His sensual laughter and the way one sloe-eyed look from him could make her go breathless with desire and wanting.

She absently pressed a hand to her fluttering belly. So much had changed between them over the past weeks, in ways that Tess had only dreamed would ever be possible. Morgan had not only become her lover again, but he'd also become her friend and confidant, and that was something that had been lacking in her life since she'd left him eight years ago. It made her truly realize what she'd given up and had her questioning how she was going to walk away from him once again.

With a deep sigh that brought her no easy answers, she walked through the big house, strolling from room to room and taking in all the new changes while thinking about Marsha's comment about turning the place into a bed and breakfast. Tess considered the place from the Realtor's perspective, and felt a shimmer of excitement ripple through her at just how much potential the house held—not for a would-be buyer, but for *her*.

She wondered if maybe *she* could be that person to turn this house into a bed and breakfast. The thought tumbled through her mind, the possibilities bringing a sense of adventure and optimism that felt so good and right.

She'd spent the past eight years in Atlanta, attending college and taking on odd jobs to make ends meet, then finally working as a marketing rep for a large Atlanta firm. And never once had her job given her any real pleasure or the kind of satisfaction or accomplishment that came from doing something you loved. She'd obviously never been cut out to be a citified career woman who needed to make her mark on the world and a have an affluent man on her arm.

No, that had been her grandmother's dream.

Deep in her heart Tess was, and always would be, a small-town girl who preferred a simple, uncomplicated life. One that was rich and rewarding in ways that no high-powered job or lifestyle could compete with. And, she was in love with a man who was a carpenter and worked with his hands for a living, and she knew she always would be in love with him.

She made her way back downstairs, and in the living room she found herself drawn to the hope chest that Morgan had given to her. It was so evident to her that the hope chest had been made with an abundance of love, and it hit her hard knowing what she'd walked away from all those years ago—even if she'd done so to please her grandmother. As a result, her actions had hurt Morgan deeply.

But Tess believed that Morgan had given her the hope chest for a reason now, and it wasn't because he wanted to off-load the piece of furniture. No, he'd kept it for the past eight years because he hadn't been able to let it, or her, go. Giving her this precious gift now told her so much, that maybe, hopefully, Morgan was still in love with her, too.

Her throat clogged with tears, and she knelt in front of the hope chest and opened it up. The inside was empty, of course, just waiting to be filled with hopes and dreams and all the cherished memories she'd missed out on the past eight years.

Now, she wanted to fill it with keepsakes from a lifetime spent with Morgan Kane.

She had no idea if he wanted the same thing, but she'd find out soon enough. But no matter how Morgan felt about her, there were choices she needed to make, for *herself,* and no one else. And that meant returning to

Atlanta and closing that chapter of her life, so she could begin a new one here in Wynhaven.

That bed and breakfast was going to be all hers, a way of keeping her grandmother's house and supporting herself as well. Because she just couldn't give up this place. It was her only legacy, a tie to her past, and the key to her future.

Coming back to live in Wynhaven was something she was doing for herself, even if Morgan didn't have a place for her in his heart or his life, which was a distinct possibility since he'd made her no promises since her return. But she'd seen the tenderness in his gaze, felt the emotion between them when they made love, and she had to believe in him, in them, and what she knew they could have together.

Her plan was a definite risk the whole way around, but she was so tired of playing it safe; tired of living her life the way her grandmother would want her to. She'd loved her grandmother, and even understood her reasons for pushing Tess to better herself, even if those ideals had been misplaced. But it was time that Tess lived her own life, and she wanted that future to be here in Wynhaven. With Morgan.

She just hoped that when she returned from Atlanta a few days from now, Morgan would want her as a part of his life and future, as well.

After a long day working on renovations for a church at a neighboring town, Morgan sat out on his front porch with a cold bottle of beer, a routine he'd adopted over the past five days since Tess had been gone.

Other than the brief message she'd left on his answering machine the day she'd left for Atlanta, Morgan had yet to hear from her, and that lack of communication between them was eating him up inside. She'd informed him that she had to take care of a few things in the city and that she'd talk to him soon, but for every day that passed without hearing from her his hopes were increasingly drowned out by doubts, along with a deep loss and pain that ached his soul.

It was his own damn fault for allowing his emotions to factor in to what should have been a simple and uncomplicated affair. Their relationship might have started out as a seduction, but he would have sworn that he'd felt something blossoming between them over the past few weeks—the love they'd once shared kindling into a deeper, richer, more mature kind of emotion and passion that held the exciting possibility of spanning a lifetime.

How had he misjudged every conversation, every look, and touch between them so badly?

He shook his head at being twice a fool. And it didn't help matters, or his bruised male pride, that when he'd seen Marsha Lawson a few days ago at the coffee shop in town she'd told him that Tess had come to see her about putting her grandmother's house up for sale. Morgan should have expected as much since that had been Tess's plan all along, but he would have liked to have heard that news from Tess herself, and not the Realtor anxious to bring in a big commission on the Monroe place.

Swearing beneath his breath, he finished off his beer and went back inside the house to see what he could make to eat, even though he didn't have much of an appetite. He found a frozen fried chicken dinner in the freezer and popped it into the microwave to cook, and grabbed a second beer. He was just twisting the cap off the bottle when his doorbell rang.

Not expecting any visitors and wanting to be left alone for the evening, he frowned and headed to the front door. He opened it and found Tess standing on his porch, wearing faded jeans, a pink T-shirt, and a tentative smile. All he could think of was that she was back from Atlanta to say her final good-byes before she returned to the city for good.

He braced a shoulder against the door frame and folded his arms across his chest. "You're back," he drawled, his tone giving nothing away. Not his surprise, nor the slim flicker of hope he couldn't help but feel at seeing her again.

She shifted on her sandaled feet, her soft brown eyes searching his. "I just got in, and I was hoping we could talk."

Again, he felt that sucker punch sensation to the stomach, but managed to keep his expression bland. "Sure," he said, and waved a hand toward the chairs on the porch.

Tess inhaled a deep breath, unable to bring herself to sit down when she had so much excess energy running through her veins, so she remained standing instead. Morgan didn't seem inclined to sit, either, and instead leaned against the porch railing.

She was incredibly nervous about this conversation with Morgan, and how it was going to end. She hoped she wasn't about to lose the best thing that had ever happened to her, and he wasn't giving her any clues about what he was feeling, either. It was like that first day when she'd gone to see him at his workshop, when he was reserved and his features were unreadable.

Her anxiety level rose a notch, and she struggled to keep her composure as she met his gaze. This was something she needed to see through, no matter the outcome. "I'm sorry I didn't call you while I was in Atlanta, but I had a lot of things I had to take care of and I just wanted to get everything done so I could come back to Wynhaven as soon as possible."

"So you can get your grandmother's house sold?" he asked gruffly.

"I'm not selling my grandmother's place."

He narrowed his gaze in confusion, and she allowed a small smile to ease up the corner of her mouth as she explained.

"That was my intent when I first came back to Wynhaven, and I even talked to Marsha about listing the house last week, but I realized I just can't do it."

He slid his fingers into the front pockets of his jeans, his entire demeanor guarded. "What changed your mind?"

"A lot factored into my decision. Mainly, I just can't

bring myself to let go of the house I grew up in, which gave me the only sense of stability and belonging I had after my mother passed away." She paused a moment, wondering how Morgan would take her next bit of news. "I've decided to turn my grandmother's place into a bed and breakfast."

He looked appropriately shocked. "Really?"

She nodded, though she heard the disbelief in his tone, as if he wasn't sure what to make of her announcement. "Actually, Marsha gave me the idea when she mentioned that the place would make a great bed and breakfast for people traveling through Wynhaven or visiting the town."

She came up beside Morgan and propped her hip on the railing next to him, taking whatever warmth and closeness she could get from him at the moment. "The more I thought about the idea, the more I wanted to be the person to turn the house into a bed and breakfast. I was going to sell the house because I couldn't afford to keep it and live in it alone, and this is the perfect solution for me to keep the place. I figure I'll hire a few people to help me out on a part-time basis with the guests and cleaning and upkeep, and I'll do most of the cooking and baking, which I love. It's an opportunity I just can't walk away from."

After a few silent moments he expressed what was on his mind. "You left for Atlanta once before, Tess. What makes you think Wynhaven is going to be enough for you now?"

It was a legitimate question, and she knew Morgan

was looking for some kind of reassurance from her, though she still had no idea where they stood with each other now.

"When I left for Atlanta after graduating high school, I did so for my grandmother," she said, needing him to understand her reasons for pursuing a life outside of Wynhaven all those years ago. "She wanted me to go to college and be successful, because my own mother was such a disappointment. Helen wanted more for me, and I honestly can't fault her for that, and though I have a lot of regrets about the way I left Wynhaven, and you, at the time I did what I believed was the right thing to do, even if it wasn't what *I* wanted. I was young and impressionable, and a part of me felt as though I owed my grandmother for raising me. Another part just wanted her to be proud of me and what I accomplished."

"And now?" he asked quietly.

"Now I'm ready to live my own life, for myself." Her voice was strong and filled with a renewed confidence. "I went to Atlanta and loaded up all my belongings in a U-haul, I closed out bank accounts and canceled the lease on my apartment. There were things I needed to resolve before I came back here and talked to you again. I wanted to return with that part of my life in Atlanta done and over with so I could start out fresh and new here in Wynhaven."

His eyes darkened, and his expression intensified. "What about us?"

It was time to put her heart and emotions on the line, and she prayed that they would be reciprocated. She moved to stand directly in front of Morgan, less than a foot away, and pressed her palm to his lean jaw. "The past three weeks being here in Wynhaven has made me realize that everything I've ever wanted is right here in this small town I grew up in. Especially you, Morgan." She swallowed hard, and gave him everything that made her who she was. "I love you, Morgan Kane. I never stopped loving you."

With a low groan he wrapped his arms around her waist and pulled her up against his body, hugging her tight. "God, Tess, I love you, too." Too soon he pulled back, and gently brushed away stray strands of her hair from her cheek. "I'm a handyman, Tess, a guy who works construction, and I always will be. You know I'll never be some fancy city executive with soft, manicured hands."

That he'd allow her to see this vulnerable side to him touched her deeply, but they'd always tried to be honest with each other, and she never wanted to lose that trust again. She held his wrists and ran her thumbs across his tough, work-roughened palms. "I love these hands of yours, Morgan. I love every single one of your callouses and how they feel when you run them slowly over my body. You're everything I've ever wanted, and I love you just the way you are."

She felt overwhelmed with a slew of emotions, yet there was still one thing left she needed to say to him. She looked into his handsome face, so he could see the sincerity in her eyes. "Morgan . . . I'm so sorry about the way I left you eight years ago. I swear I never deliberately meant to hurt you."

"I know, sweetheart," he said as a silent understanding passed between them, erasing the pain of the past and making room for a bright new future together. And then he framed her face in his hands and took her mouth in a kiss so hard and deep it literally lifted her off her feet.

"Marry me, Tess," he breathed once he let them both up for air again, his gaze warm and tender and his eyes shining with the same undeniable emotion bursting inside of her. "I want you to be my wife. I want to have babies with you and raise them here in Wynhaven, and I want to grow old with you. I don't want a day to pass without you in it."

"Yes," she shouted exuberantly, wanting all that with Morgan, too. "Yes, yes, *yes!*"

A small frown furrowed Morgan's brows, though his eyes sparkled with that southern charm of his she'd missed so much. "Except we have a little problem."

She stared up at him, wide-eyed and curious, certain after how far they'd come they could work out any issues left between them. "What's that?"

"You're going to have to hire someone to stay at the bed and breakfast full-time, because you'll be in *my* bed every single night."

She grinned, feeling his strong heart beat beneath the hands she'd rested on his chest. "I don't see that as a problem."

"Good." He swept her up in his arms and headed for the front door. "Then you'll be sleeping in my bed from tonight on."

She laughed joyfully. As he carried her to his bedroom, laid her on the big four poster bed, and spent the next hour making love to her with those slow, talented hands of his, Tess knew she'd come home for good.

COLOR
ME WICKED

Nina Bangs

◆ PROLOGUE

"Sensational sex with a wicked twist isn't a slam-dunk, Deimos. Trust me, I know. You're talking to a maven of sensual meddling here, and manipulation is my heart, my soul, my . . . Fine, so I'm not into hearts and souls, but you get the idea." Sparkle Stardust crossed her legs and shifted her bottom into a more comfortable position as she perched on the stool behind her candy counter.

Deimos didn't look impressed. *"I'm a cosmic troublemaker just like you. What you can do, I can do, too."*

"But I can do it better, babe. You're getting a chance to learn from the best. Specialization is where it's at, and my unique talent lies in hooking up couples who're, well, completely wrong for each other. If I'm lucky, they hate each other. I use my immense power to drag them, er . . . guide them gently toward sexual nirvana. I decided to mentor you because I sensed your deep well of untapped potential for creating sexual mayhem. So how does that work for you?"

Ignoring the hem of her black dress that slithered higher up her thigh with each wiggle, she frowned at her toenails exposed by fuchsia Jimmy Choo sandals with six-inch heels. Her fave shoes. They made a statement: I'm hot, armed, and dangerous. Great shoes created a positive work environment. "Chipped polish alert. Remind me to do my toenails tonight. Perfect nail color feeds my emotional well-being."

Deimos offered her a sulky glare. He crouched in all his feline splendor on the sill of the store's front window. He'd chosen to take the form of an Ocicat, a domestic cat that looked like a miniature leopard. She applauded his visual impact and wild dramatic appearance. He looked like he'd just stepped out of the jungle.

"It doesn't work at all. Cosmic troublemakers are supposed to spread chaos throughout the universe. Solar explosions that fry planets, Planet X collisions that pulverize unsuspecting worlds, ice ages that freeze whole continents—really big important stuff like that. And I don't care about sex or your damn toes." He lifted his lips in a silent snarl. *"And why the hell do I have to be a cat?"*

"Mmm. Such passionate aggression. I love it. Bad attitudes are sexy." Sparkle laid both palms flat on the glass counter-top and studied her nails. "When did you come into being, Deimos?" Maybe she'd try a different nail color, a deep, sensual shade of red. "What do you think, should I change colors? Maybe I'll try Dark Desire. It gives me yummy shivers just saying its name. I can almost feel the cool slide of it on my nails, see the intense rich shine of it—"

"Two thousand one, and I don't give a damn about—"

Sparkle sighed. "I know, you don't give a damn about my nails. You know, you need to seriously get in touch with your senses." She studied him. His lithe cat body fairly thrummed with impatience. So young, so reckless, so *stupid.* "I'm going to lay everything out for you. First off, it doesn't take any talent to destroy inanimate objects. They don't argue or say no. Messing with human emotions is the real challenge. People never do what you expect them to do."

"So what's your point?" Deimos yawned to demonstrate his complete lack of interest in messing with human emotions. *"You still haven't told me why I have to be a cat. And why can't I talk out loud?"*

Now he was really starting to tick her off. "Look, I've been around for thousands of years, and I have power you can only dream about. So my point is, if I chose to mentor you, then you damn well better get with the program."

She read the mutinous darkening of his amber eyes, the angry twitch of his tail. Her kick-butt approach wasn't getting the job done. Maybe she needed to appeal to his ego. Males, whether human or nonhuman, were Silly Putty in the hands of a smart woman who knew how to stroke their egos.

Sparkle transformed her expression into her favorite persona: the sensual seductress. She'd practiced and perfected it over the centuries. Now she aimed it at the mini jungle-kitty glaring at her from across the store.

"Come here, cutie." She crooked her finger at him.

He padded over to the counter.

"Sit here." She indicated the chair next to him that she always kept ready for any male customer, usually elderly, who grew weak from exposure to all of her erotic intensity.

Deimos leaped for the chair, a soaring graceful arc that fell about three inches short of his target. He managed to hook his front paws onto the seat and hung there with back paws treading air. Sparkle leaned across the counter, grabbed the back of his neck, and lifted him onto the seat. "Your eye-paw coordination is still a little off, but it'll get better." A lie. He was a klutz.

Before he had a chance to whine, Sparkle scratched behind his ears and then slid her fingers the length of his back. She felt him relax beneath her touch. "I chose you out of all the newbie cosmic troublemakers because I saw the possibility for greatness in you, Deimos. And all of the most famous cosmic troublemakers have taken cat forms at one time or another. Cats are beautiful, intelligent, and deliciously sneaky. Perfect for spying. I bet you'll make an incredible spy."

Deimos blinked as the anger faded from his eyes. *"Yeah?"* If he wasn't careful, his expanding pride would puff him up like a balloon, and he'd just float away. *"I'll have to communicate mentally so no one catches on that I'm a spy."*

Sparkle smiled. "Yeah." But then her smile wavered. "You're lucky I let you choose your cat form. I was forced to be a white cat." She allowed herself a delicate shudder. "White made my butt look huge. It scarred my psyche for months."

She ignored Deimos's blank look and continued to stroke him. "Only a special few have the talent to impact human lives on a personal level. As soon as I saw you, I knew you were one of the few. You're immensely gifted and have this amazing sexual aura. It just blew me away."

Deimos practically glowed. *"For real? I won't let you down. I'll work my tail off. What's your plan?"*

Gotcha. "Here's the deal. For thousands of years I've served up sex and sin for dessert, so owning a candy store seemed a natural progression. I bought Sweet Indulgence, my little shop of chocolate creams and erotic dreams, because it was next to this Disney World wannabe. I figured that thousands of people would pour into Galveston to visit the theme park, and I'd have lots of potential victims to scope out."

Deimos washed his face with one spotted paw. *"Makes sense."*

"Uh-uh. Didn't work out. The only ones who walked through my door were young couples trailing their two point five sticky-fingered kiddies after them. They were so not the clientele I'd hoped for." It hadn't taken long for her to realize she'd either have to sell her store or get rid of the theme park.

"So I had my attorney buy the park. I've renamed it Live the Fantasy, and I envision a reality theme park where adults can role-play wild adventures. Always wanted to be the captain of a pirate ship? You've got it at Live the Fantasy. The park is G rated, so the city fathers expect everyone to have good clean fun." Her smile was filled with wicked intent. "They're kidding, right? How boring is that? The only good fantasy is a sexual fantasy. I get yummy shivers just thinking about the lust a few intense fantasies will generate." Sparkle felt tingly all over, the reaction of a true sexual visionary. "I foresee thousands of people jump-starting their sputtering sex lives after a visit to Live the Fantasy."

Deimos's whiskers twitched with excitement. *"Wow, sounds great. Hey, when you get bored with the whole theme park thing, can I level it with a tsunami?"*

Sparkle didn't have the heart to crush all that hopeful puppy dog eagerness. "We'll see."

She glanced down at the old Ball High yearbook she'd been studying before Deimos showed up. "I'm getting ready to transform the Happy Castle into the Castle of Dark Dreams. I was in the middle of choosing someone to do the exterior and interior painting, and then I have to pick an interior designer. I'll have my lawyer do the actual hiring. I don't want anyone to know I own the park."

Deimos put his front paws on the counter so he could peer at the book. *"Anyone special in mind?"*

Sparkle slid the tip of her tongue across her lower lip. Oh, yessss. She got all shivery with anticipation at the sensual world of possibilities ahead. "I have two people who'll be perfect for the jobs. I'm about to turn up the heat in our little fantasy park and see what burns."

CHAPTER ◆ ONE

"What a wonderful blending of form and function. It projects an aura of towering strength with an intriguing touch of dark and dangerous." Sparkle Stardust swept her arms wide to emphasize her opinion of the Castle of Dark Dreams. Her cat crouched beside her, his unblinking gaze proclaiming that he was bored, bored, bored.

"No kidding." Amanda Harcourt was more focused on specifics than Sparkle. She stared across the moat. A man stood on a short ladder painting trim around the outer-wall gate. His back was to them.

Form and function. Mmm. A wonderful form. And said form was functioning very well as far as she could see. He'd stripped to the waist in the blazing June sun and his worn jeans hugged every line of his firm butt and long legs. Fascinated, she watched the flow of muscles beneath bronzed skin as he made smooth, even strokes with his brush.

Dark and dangerous? Worked for her. The light breeze lifted his dark hair from his neck. Hair that was a little too long and a little too shaggy. Sexy elemental male vibes shimmered off him in waves.

During the ten years she'd spent in New York honing her interior designing skills, she'd had plenty of opportunities to hook up with a fair sampling of the city's male population. Major disappointments. But maybe now that she was back home in Galveston for a while, she'd dip her toe into the hot and oh-so-alpha Texas male pool. She deserved some fun.

"He has a sensual quality that goes with the castle, doesn't he?" Sparkle sounded amused.

Amanda blinked and looked at Sparkle. "What?"

"Your sexy painter." Sparkle's amber eyes gleamed with sly knowledge. "Hey, I understand."

Okay, now Amanda was officially embarrassed. She'd spent ten years stomping the old Amanda Harcourt into submission and rebuilding her business and personal image into the one her wealthy clients loved—cool and in control. She was sophisticated-hip. No emotional artistic phoniness for her. And she paid attention to details. A calm casual elegance gave her clients confidence in her. She was wearing a cream sleeveless dress today because light neutrals were her favorite colors. That hadn't always been true, but neutrals fed people's perception of her, and perception was everything.

Cool, elegant, and in control didn't ogle painters, at least not during working hours.

But something told her a lie wouldn't fool Sparkle. "I've been away from Texas too long. I forgot how much heat Texas guys can generate." She shrugged and smiled. "If I need to stare, I should walk across Sea Wall Boulevard and go down to the beach. I'll find plenty of buff bods wearing a lot less."

"I guess." Sparkle looked doubtful. "But they won't have his sizzle." She studied the buff bod with the brush. "Look at him—yummy broad shoulders, and that muscular back gleaming with a light sheen of sweat. Doesn't it make you feel all prickly to think about trailing your fingers over his warm bare skin?" She fixed Amanda with an unblinking stare that had the same feline intensity as her pet. "There's nothing more arousing than watching a strong man working a well-toned body. It's that primitive need every woman has to take the most physically powerful male into her bed and—"

"Oh, wow." Amanda glanced at her watch. "I've taken up all of your lunch hour. I really appreciate you taking time to show me the park, but I guess you have to get back to your store now." *Please have to get back to your store.*

Sparkle offered her an exaggerated sigh as she pushed her long red hair away from her face. "I suppose I should get back, but I'll let Deimos tag along with you. He loves snooping around in the castle." She glanced down at the spotted cat before raising her gaze once again to Amanda. "No one knows who owns the park. Everything goes through the lawyer. I've helped him out a few times, because I'm the neighborly type. But I'm curious about all the secrecy. Are you supposed to meet the owner here?"

Amanda frowned at the cat, and the cat stared intently back at her. Wasn't Sparkle afraid her cat would run into the street? "No, but the attorney should be here any minute now. I've never spoken to the owner." Didn't the cat ever blink?

"Hmm, strange. Well, have fun, sister." Sparkle's smile said the fun she had in mind didn't have anything to do with decorating. "And don't worry, Deimos won't go into the street."

A cosmic coincidence. They'd both been thinking about the cat wandering into the street at the same time. Amanda watched Sparkle walk away, although "walk" didn't say it at all. Her swing and sway said "man-catcher" loud and clear. Amanda spent a few seconds pondering the aesthetics of Sparkle's black shorts and black clingy top. Sure they were sexy, but . . . Amanda did a few mental head-shakes to clear away the weirdness that had accumulated over the last few days.

Why had she dropped everything to take this job? Good grief, she'd left New York to decorate a *castle*. What did she know about decorating castles? And who really had a name like Sparkle Stardust? Amanda must've tripped and fallen headfirst into Alice's rabbit hole.

Without permission, her gaze drifted back to the hunky painter. There were other people working on the castle, but none so visually stimulating. She strolled across the drawbridge. His front probably wouldn't be able to live up to the promise of his back. Two halves didn't usually add up to one awesome whole.

But hey, that was okay, because she needed to focus on her job and nothing else. Mentally plunking her professional glasses on her nose, she studied the castle. Pretty ordinary as castles went. From her brief research, it looked like it was a mixture of several different time periods—a keep with four square towers, and a curtain wall.

The lawyer had said the great hall and a few other areas would be used for role-playing. The rest of the castle would be for guest rooms, a restaurant, and several shops. She'd never decorated the real deal, but there had to be a first time for everything. Before leaving New York, she'd done a mad research scramble, but had only skimmed the surface.

Uh-oh. Something was wrong with her professional perspective. As her gaze slid back to The Painter, her glasses morphed into sexy shades, perfect for fun in the sun and viewing bright celestial bodies. *Bodies*. Amanda sighed her defeat. Curiosity, the Harcourt curse, wouldn't let her concentrate on the castle until she saw his front. So be it.

Amanda refused to sneak. If New York had taught her anything, it was that you boldly and aggressively pursued your goal. She strode to within a few feet of his ladder and gazed up. So big, so tanned, so authentically male. No research needed to figure that out.

She narrowed her gaze on his broad back. New York
had also taught her how to be devious. "Umm, who's in
charge of your paint crew? I need to talk to your boss
about—"

"I own the paint company, so I guess you've found
the boss." His voice was a husky and darkly compelling
promise that he indeed would *always* be the boss.

"Oh. Well, I . . ." Wait. She frowned. There was
something familiar about that voice. A deeper and more
sensual echo of a voice she'd once known. Dawning
horror widened her eyes as the man stepped off the ladder and turned to face her.

She knew him. Knew that hard face with those light
hazel eyes framed by thick dark lashes. Knew the sensual mouth that enhanced his bad-boy image. She hadn't
forgotten anything. Not the three-inch scar on his thigh
he'd earned while playing running back for Ball High,
nor the tattoo on his hip.

"Mandy?" His voice was erotic promise and unspoken lies.

Like lemmings, women always swam out way too far
in his sea of sensual promises and then drowned in those
lies. Not her, of course. Never her.

"Conleth Maguire." Saying his whole name dis-
tanced her from him, and she needed all the distance she
could get. A few hundred miles minimum.

"What dragged you back home, wicked woman?"
His smile was slow, welcoming, and a sensual minefield
for the unwary. And because she was *not* unwary, she re-

alized she needed to say something quick to diffuse the power of that smile.

"Lots of money. The owner hired me to decorate the castle." Home? Amanda had tried for years to reprogram her subconscious to believe New York was home. But standing here staring at Con tugged at something she thought she'd left behind ten years ago.

"Money. Figures." His smile didn't waver, but the warmth in those incredible eyes cooled just a little.

What was wrong with money? Money was good. It bought acceptance, love. Okay, maybe not love, but certainly a sincere level of caring. She took a deep breath to renew her brain's oxygen supply. She'd better say something fast before mutually uncomfortable memories filled up the void.

"So what color scheme did the owner decide to go with for the exterior?" Why hadn't she noticed the color of the trim he was painting? Because you were too busy wiping the drool off your chin, stupid. If she looked now, she'd have to take her eyes off Maguire. Not a good idea.

Con shrugged. "I get to choose my own colors." He glanced at her dress, stripped her down to bare essentials with his heated stare, and proclaimed her wanting. "I don't like neutrals." Capturing her gaze, he slowly rubbed his hand across his chest. "I like colors that burn for me."

He'd done that on purpose, the jerk. He thought he'd sidetrack her professional questions by drawing her attention to his chest. His broad muscular chest with dark male nipples and a light scattering of hair damp from his exertions. Of course, he'd failed, because she hadn't noticed at all.

Colors that burn for me. What exactly did he mean by that? She'd ask, but any question with the word *burn* in it was bound to send her skipping merrily down the wicked path Con hoped she'd follow. Uh-uh, she was smarter than that.

What to say? She'd try the time-honored Galveston icebreaker, "Do you think Hurricane Billy Bob will come into the Gulf?" but Con would manage to make something sexual out of the hurricane, too. She'd be safer sticking to a few professional statements. "I—"

"I bet you're getting ready to ask if anything's new with me. Not much. I still have the rose tattoo. No wife and kids. And I own a condo about a block away." His smile widened, immediately taking her back to her teen years. "Do you still have the little blue butterfly on your behind?"

"My behind is none of your business, Maguire. It hasn't been for a long time." She stared at a point somewhere beyond his left shoulder. Did he remember the body decorations of all the women he'd had sex with? Nah. No human had that kind of memory storage capacity.

He lowered his gaze to her general butterfly area. "That butterfly brings back great memories."

He was smoke, fire, and unresolved dreams. Always had been. She needed a firewall. Breaking eye contact, she rooted through the items thrown pell-mell into her Gucci purse. A purse with that brand name deserved better, but her purse was the one part of her life she'd never managed to organize.

"Hey, I'm glad you and your rose are still together. Personally, I don't remember it." She didn't look up as she continued to root.

All right, so she also had problems stuffing memories of Con and his tattoo into a neat compartment, but at least while she was in New York she didn't have to face him in the flesh. In the flesh? Nope, wouldn't go there. Ah, her sunglasses. She pulled them from the rubble and put them on. There. No windows to the soul showing. Now she could safely present her cool and in-control face.

He shook his head and offered her a fake frown. "Ouch. That hurt, sweet-heat. All these years I imagined you lusting after my tattoo."

"I don't lust, Con. Not now, not ever." Well, maybe the not ever part wasn't the absolute truth, but Amanda felt the moment called for sweeping statements of denial. "And don't call me sweet-heat. I'm not that person anymore, haven't been for ten years." She wasn't thrilled with being Mandy or wicked woman again either, but she'd choose her battles.

He nodded, his expression turning thoughtful. Reaching back to the ladder, he picked up a cloth and wiped a few spots of paint from his hands.

Amanda forced away thoughts of what wonders those strong hands could work. "Let's get back to the castle. I think—"

"Whoa." He held up his hand to stop her. "I want to discuss this not remembering the black rose thing. Your relation to my tattoo was a cornerstone of my youthful fantasies."

His smile returned warmer, more intimate. Reminding her of exactly where she'd been and what they'd been doing when she'd seen the tattoo for the first and only time.

Okay, time to take a stand. "I'm here for only one thing, to decorate this castle. I don't want to talk about your tattoo or your fantasies."

"Or your part in them?" He shoved the paint cloth into the back pocket of his jeans as he moved closer to her. "Amazing what we choose not to remember about another person's body."

What do you remember about my body? No, not a safe question. She was safer sticking to *his* body. Amanda had always appreciated fine artwork, in any form. And Con's black rose was a great visual. Not the biggest or the best to be seen on the Body-Maguire, but still great.

Amanda sighed. He wasn't going to leave the rose alone. The best she could do was to steer the discussion away from the personal. "Why a rose? Men don't usually tattoo flowers on their bodies. Guess it threatens their masculinity." He could've covered his body with flowers and never put a dent in his virility. It oozed from his pores.

He moved even closer, invading her personal space. "I never told you the story behind the rose, did I? But then we weren't into lengthy explanations that night, were we, Mandy?" Reaching out, he calmly removed her sunglasses. His gaze moved leisurely over her body and then lifted to lock with her eyes. "If I concentrate, I can still feel the slide of your tongue as you traced the rose." He lowered his gaze, his lashes hiding his expression. "Lots of heat and tactile sensations. A man doesn't forget that kind of experience." He handed the sunglasses to her.

Amanda sucked in her breath. Whoa, losing control of the conversation here. What should she say . . . ?

He laughed. Low, husky, and with the sensual warmth that had always been part of Conleth Maguire. "Relax. We won't share any more tongue memories. I just wanted to see if you could still blush, or if New York had taken all of Galveston out of you. The blush is still there, but the big city sure changed a lot of other things." He reached out and slid his fingers through her hair.

Her *blond* hair. She loved her hair. And she hated how effortlessly he could bring the heat to her face. But then, he'd always been able to bring heat to any part of her body he chose.

"Too bad if you don't like it." She visualized the blush fading from her face leaving her cooly elegant and impervious to anything Conleth Maguire might do or say. Amanda hadn't come home to be haunted by a ghost-of-lover-past.

He widened his eyes, a weak attempt to look innocent. Con didn't do innocent well. "Did I say I didn't like your hair? I love your hair."

Ha! He hated her hair. Con lied with eyes wide open. Always had, and she didn't think ten years had changed him. "Are you going to tell me why you chose this rose tattoo that I definitely don't remember?" Once he got the rose explanation out of his system, she'd try to segue into talking about the job.

He nodded and motioned her into the shade of the castle's wall. "*Roisin Dubh* means dark rose in Irish. Legend says that it was a Druid symbol. The Council of the *Roisin Dubh* wore the black rose on their robes."

She nodded as she leaned one shoulder against the castle wall and blessed the small relief the shade gave her. "Got it. A bunch of Druids took the rose as their symbol. I never realized you were into mystic stuff." Where was the attorney? She needed to extricate herself from this conversation before it dove deeper into the personal.

"There're lots of things you never realized, sweetheart." Beneath the seemingly sensual suggestion, anger lurked. "Too bad you didn't stick around long enough to find out."

He'd thrown down the gauntlet. This was *not* what she'd planned for her first day on the new job. She could turn and walk away from the confrontation, but experience had taught her that she who turns and leaves the room is often booted in the behind on the way out. Uh-uh. He wanted reaction, and he'd get it. She moved away from the wall's support.

"Fine. Let's deal with this now and get it out of the way. We went out during my senior year. We planned to go to New York together. You'd go to art school, and I'd learn interior design. We had sex for the first time a week before I graduated. The next day you told me you'd changed your mind. You were staying in Galveston and going to work for your father. No other explanation. Did I miss anything?" She offered him a careless shrug that said it was a non-event to her now. "So what's a girl to think?" She'd thought a lot. Maybe after making love with her, he'd lost interest. Had he found someone else? The list went on and on. The bottom line? He hadn't cared.

It amazed Con that at five feet, four inches, Mandy could stand so tall. Those wide blue eyes might say vulnerable, but they were dead wrong. They were a holdover from the girl she'd been when she left Galveston. The woman who faced him now would give as good as she got. He liked that. Con wondered what she'd do if he reached down and ruffled that smooth short hair. Probably haul off and sock him.

But hair-ruffling could wait. He needed to give her the explanation he hadn't given her ten years ago. If they had to work together, he didn't want the past getting in the way.

"I didn't have the money to go to New York with you." He winced. Even after all the years, it hurt to admit the truth.

"What?"

He'd shocked her. Good. Con didn't know why, but he enjoyed taking her out of her comfort zone, her perception of the world according to Amanda Harcourt.

"Dad had said he'd help with my tuition. When he found out I wanted to go to New York, he took back his offer. Said I didn't have to go all the way to New York to learn how to scribble pictures."

"Why didn't you tell me?" Her eyes darkened. With hurt, anger? He wasn't sure.

"What would you have done if I'd told you?" He knew the answer, but he wanted to hear her say it.

"I could've lent you the money. My parents . . ." She trailed off. "That's why you didn't tell me."

Con nodded. She knew too well the eighteen-year-old he'd been. But she didn't know the man he'd become. "I always had too much pride." He smiled "Still do. Back then, I thought your anger was preferable to your pity."

"Would you still do the same thing today?" She sounded casual, but Con sensed his answer was a little more important than she wanted it to be.

"Probably." He paused to give her time to think about it. "I'd tell a different lie this time around, though."

She nodded as though it all made perfect sense. "Thanks for telling me. I was just a kid back then, and with hormone levels spiking, I spent a whole week either crying or thinking up painful ways to end your life."

A week. And then she'd gone on with her life. But he'd gone on with his life, too. They were even. Then why did he still feel that unreasonable stab of anger when he thought about her ten years in New York?

"I'm glad we got that out of the way. Gee, I'm probably late for my meeting." Her expression said she hoped he'd disappear in a puff of smoke.

He wouldn't make it that easy for her. "I didn't finish telling you about the family Druids. Dad's always been obsessed with his Irish roots. There's no real proof, but he's convinced our family has a few Druid connections." Con could feel her need to escape him, but a part of him that stubbornly resisted maturity wanted to see her squirm. He'd make her wait out his explanation. "Back then, I thought it was pretty cool that I might be related to an ancient society with a dark and mysterious reputation."

Con thought she'd offer him a polite smile. Instead, she gripped her bottom lip between small white teeth and studied him. His primitive part in charge of sexual awareness growled its pleasure. And when she released that lip . . . just the sight of the full damp sheen of it upped the growl to a roar. His reactions were right on schedule. If he remembered the spectacular event they'd shared on a moonlit Galveston beach correctly, and he thought he did, every breath Amanda Harcourt took had been a turn-on to his testosterone-driven younger self. The scary part was that she was having the same effect now on his older experienced self.

"You never needed any Druid relatives, Con. Every girl at Ball High not only thought you were dark and mysterious, but the hottest hottie of them all." She firmed her lips, a sure indication of a serious pronouncement, and proof positive that her lips were sexy in whatever shape she chose to bend them. "But that's past history. We're two different people now. Once I've made a final decision on the colors, I'll consult with you about your painting schedule for the interior of the castle. We'll consult about the castle, *nothing else*."

Strange. Why hire a New York designer when Houston had plenty of great ones? He nodded. "Sure. And wicked woman, maybe you consult in New York, but down here in Galveston we talk." Why was he so steamed? She'd walked away from here ten years ago and never looked back. Amanda Harcourt didn't matter anymore. Other than mutual lust, they'd never had anything in common.

"Can we lose the wicked woman?" Her semi-smile said she was a little conflicted about him and searching for something neutral to say. From her smooth cap of blond hair down to her cream dress and sandals, it looked like she'd cornered the market on neutral.

"I guess your dad's happy you became a painter. I mean, he always wanted his children to be part of the construction business." Translation: you caved and did what Daddy wanted you to do.

He thought about telling her he'd taken art courses in Houston but decided to keep quiet. She didn't care what he'd done with his life.

Her gaze slid away from him. "Maybe I'll look inside just in case the attorney slipped into the castle through another entrance."

Mandy started to walk past him and then froze. She stared at the trim he'd been painting. *"Red?"*

Con imagined the word *plague* would drip off her

tongue with exactly the same tone. "It's a little more than just red, but yeah, it's red." Something evil in him sensed the color was an abomination to her and it reveled in her disgust. "I like red. I'm pretty sure I'll paint almost everything in the castle red."

"Inside?" She vibrated with outrage.

Obviously, she thought the park's owner had just hired him to slap paint on the castle. Obviously, she thought she'd get to choose all the colors. Surprise, surprise. The evil in him rubbed its hands together and gleefully plunged onward. "Uh-huh. I like lime green and neon orange, too. So don't worry, I won't paint everything red."

"No." The word was a breathy exhalation of defiance. "You will *not* use those colors. I'm the designer—"

She got no further. At that moment the cat must've decided to take a closer look at this paint that was causing such a brouhaha, and leaped for the ladder where the small can rested.

Con's last coherent thought as he watched the cat scrabble for purchase with its front paws on the shelf holding the paint, was that he'd never seen such an uncoordinated animal in his life. Reflexively, he reached for the paint. Too late. Frantic to keep from falling to the ground, the cat hooked the can with one paw and brought it down on top him as he lost the battle with gravity.

"Ohmigod!" Mandy's wail of disbelief was echoed by the cat's yowl of surprise.

Red paint coated the cat from whiskers to tail. He

was Dynamic-Red highlighted by gleaming yellow eyes. The cat expressed his general feelings with furious hisses and growls. He was one pissed kitty.

"Get this crap off me now! I don't have a freakin' public humiliation clause in my contract."

Startled, Con glanced around. Someone talking in his head? Nah. He shrugged away the momentary weirdness and leaped into action.

Before the cat had a chance to race away, he scooped it up like a fumble recovery and ran with it. The cat fought him as Mandy shouted advice, but he kept running until he reached the edge of the moat. Maintaining a secure grip on the cat, he knelt and then dipped it into the water.

The cat screeched and clawed. Con was aware that Mandy had scrambled down beside him. He glanced at her. "I'll hold him while you wash the paint off."

"Me?" She sounded horrified.

Probably thought red hands didn't make the right color statement for her. "Look, do you want to be the one to return him to Sparkle looking like a *Texas Chain Saw Massacre* survivor?"

Mandy widened those big blue eyes, and for just a moment he was back on the beach all those years ago. There'd been a full moon reflecting off the Gulf that night. He'd parked his pickup high on the beach, and then they'd walked hand in hand down to the water. They'd knelt on the sand facing each other, and she'd looked at him out of those same eyes. But back then her eyes had shone with sensual hunger, and he'd been generating enough lust to power all of Texas.

She broke the brief spell by glancing down at the struggling cat. "You're right. I'll rinse off the paint. Don't let him go."

Easier said than done. Hanging on to the damned cat was like holding onto a greased pig with claws. The cat was still twisting and yowling. Someone had probably already called 911 to report a murder in progress.

"Help! Cat drowner! Don't even think about dunking my head. I can't feel the bottom. I have to feel the bottom! I can't swim, you jerk. Land. Put me on land before I turn you into a small ugly parasite."

It had to be the heat. He'd been painting in the sun for too long today. Once the cat was taken care of, he'd go into the castle, cool off, and eat lunch. So why hadn't he heard voices on other days when he worked in the heat? He didn't want to think about it. He had to believe it was the heat, or accept that the cat was talking to him. And that would spell certifiable with a capital C.

Finally, between the two of them, the cat was clean. Con set it on the bank expecting it to race for home. Instead, it carefully shook each paw free of water and then glowered at them.

Con frowned as he pulled a clean rag from his back pocket and handed it to her. "Dad's a dog man, so we never had any cats at home, but I'd swear what we're seeing here isn't normal cat behavior. Look, it's not running away. It's just glaring at us." He glanced at Mandy. Uh-oh. She was dabbing at red paint spots on her dress.

"It's not glaring at *us*. It's glaring at that red trim. Cats have more sophisticated tastes than dogs. A dog would like red trim. A cat knows better."

Con didn't try to hide his grin. She sounded ticked off, and ticked off could be a prelude to other emotions. Anything that got Mandy all passionate about something had to be an improvement over her Princess of Perfect persona. "I don't know. Seems strange to me that he doesn't act more frightened." Absently, Con rubbed some paint splatters from his arms and chest.

Mandy didn't look any less furious, but her gaze never left his hand. He accommodated her by sliding the cloth over his skin more slowly, finding spots to touch low on his stomach. He would've found even more interesting places to rub if he felt she'd believe paint could've reached there.

"My family *did* have cats, so I'll clue you in on a cat fact. Cats get even. Deimos won't forget that you dunked him in the water, and when you least expect it he'll . . . well, just watch your back, Maguire." There was a hint of gleeful satisfaction in her voice.

"Deimos?" He laughed as he turned toward her. "What kind of cat name is Deimos?"

The cat hissed at him, but he ignored Deimos as he looked at Mandy's shoes. Great. Just great. Her shoes were spattered with Dynamic-Red, too. At least the color matched the temper he saw simmering in her eyes.

"I'm sorry about your dress. Make sure I get the cleaning bill." He sensed she felt he hadn't offered nearly enough compensation. Maybe he should offer his head. Not a good idea. She might take him up on it. "Let's go into the castle. I can at least clean up your shoes."

Her narrowed gaze said that Deimos wasn't the only one who wouldn't forget this. "Fine. But I don't have time to change. How will I explain this to Mr. Holgarth?" She gestured at her paint-spattered dress.

A polite cough drew their attention to the drawbridge and the man standing there.

"You will simply explain that you always sweat blood for your employer. An admirable employee trait, I'm sure." The man strode to them and offered his hand to an openmouthed Mandy. "I'm Holgarth, and you are Ms. Harcourt, I assume."

"Yes, I'm—"

"You're late, Ms. Harcourt. I do insist on punctuality. So if you must play in the water, please refrain from doing it on company time. Now, if you'll follow me, we'll go inside where it's cooler." Without waiting for a reply, he turned and walked toward the castle.

From where Con stood, it seemed like Mandy's eyes took up half her face as she turned to look at him.

"Tell me he's not dressed like a wizard."

CHAPTER ◆ TWO

"A wizard with a law degree? Scary concept. What does he do if a jury doesn't buy his closing argument?" Amanda stared at Holgarth's back as he led them across the outer courtyard. "No, don't tell me. I don't want to know." She paused as Holgarth approached the massive castle doors. Con and Deimos stopped beside her.

Amanda would keep concentrating on Holgarth. She would *not* think about Con's explanation for what he'd done ten years ago. The past had to stay in the past.

Con pulled his black T-shirt over his head, covering that yummy chest. "He's a lawyer. He's a wizard. He multitasks. What's the big deal? Oh, and your jury question? I think we're talking a sudden jump in the frog population."

She looked to see if Con was laughing. He wasn't. "You're kidding, right?" Amanda glanced down at the

cat who looked back at her with a contemptuous unblinking stare. "And what's with you, cat? Why're you
still here?" Deimos didn't deign to answer.

Con moved closer, touching her with heat and his remembered scent. Oooh yes, it was all coming back to
her now, along with the wonder of his black rose. Taking
a deep breath, she moved away from him. She didn't
need to be anywhere near the sexual force field he created so easily.

"Holgarth was wearing that blue robe and pointed hat
the first time I met him. He said he was a wizard, and as
long as he keeps paying me, he can be the tooth fairy for
all I care. Hey, I'm open to all kinds of possibilities."
Con speared her with an intent stare. "See, we have
something in common. We both agree it's all about the
money. But as far as possibilities go, you need to be way
more flexible."

Amanda shrugged away a momentary twinge of
guilt. She'd sort of lied about the money thing. If she
were really honest with herself, she'd admit it was about
acceptance. Everything in her life had been about acceptance. And coming back to her hometown to do a
high profile job like this was the ultimate feel-good moment. She'd never admit that to anyone. Most of the
time she didn't even admit it to herself.

"I'm not inflexible. I'm just focused on my goals.
And wizards don't fit into my career planning." She narrowed her gaze on Holgarth, the walking stereotype.
Sheesh, he even had glittery suns, moons, and stars on
his tall conical hat. Amanda blinked as he pulled what

looked like a wand from beneath the folds of his robe. "Is that a wand or a new kind of mosquito whacker?"

Con didn't have a chance to answer. Holgarth raised his wand and a crack of thunder shattered the perfectly sunny day. The castle doors swung open and Holgarth swept inside with a majestic swish of his robes. He didn't glance behind him to see if they followed.

Amanda did some mental eye-rolls. Give me a break. So the castle had a few neat special effects. Once inside, she turned in a slow circle, trying not to be impressed by what she assumed was the great hall. The vaulted ceiling, the huge fireplace, the raised platform for the lord's table. Yes, the room had lots of potential. And thank the gods of good taste, there was no red, lime green, or neon orange anywhere in the room. Just pristine white walls. It was Con-free for the moment, and she intended to keep it that way.

"I didn't need the wand, you know," Holgarth said.

"What?" She turned to look at him.

"I do so enjoy a dramatic moment, but I really didn't need a wand to create the thunder or open the doors." He slowly stroked his long pointed beard while he watched her.

She'd just bet he practiced long and hard on his piercing stare. So many little kids to scare, so little time. Thin, short, and gray-haired, with lips that looked like they were perpetually pursed, Holgarth needed an Extreme Makeover to capture the now wizardy look.

Con joined her. "Look, Holgarth, Mandy and I have to know the rules. I don't think we share the same vision for this place. Who's in charge of what? And why can't we talk to the owner?"

Holgarth looked down his long nose at both of them. This must be his you-are-dirt-beneath-my-platform-shoes stare. Amanda waited expectantly for his eyes to cross.

"The owner wishes to remain anonymous. He, she, or possibly it has put me in charge of seeing that the readying of the castle runs smoothly." He waved his hand in a dismissive gesture. "I can't be bothered with minor details. Work things out between you." Once again, he glanced at his watch. "I'm interviewing candidates to manage the castle. The owner wants three of them—heaven knows why—and insists they be 'more than men.' Do you know how hard it is to get *any* good help nowadays let alone find ones who are 'more than men?'"

He offered a long-suffering sigh. "But I live to serve, so I'll start interviewing. Oh, I have the key to your room. I'm so glad you chose to stay in the castle." He searched beneath the folds of his robe.

Was he for real? Amanda hoped not. "What choice do I have? You wrote it into the contract."

"A dedicated employee would always choose to be on call. Southeast tower, fourth floor. It's the Sleeping Princess room. I'll have someone get your luggage from your car and bring it up to you. The owner intends to rename all the rooms, but for now we must suffer. If you wish to purchase anything, Ms. Harcourt, you may charge it to the park." He handed her a large old-fashioned-looking key. *That* would keep the bad guys out. Not.

Turning his back on them, he hurried away leaving Amanda with her mouth open ready to ask the first of her, oh say, five hundred questions.

Disbelieving, she turned to Con. "I don't get it. Do you get it?" Amanda didn't give him a chance to answer. "How can this work? We don't even have the same tastes. In anything." Well, maybe in one thing, but sexual compatibility wouldn't help them agree on wall colors. She threw him a baleful glare. "I'm not even sure you *have* any taste. What kind of owner sits back and lets the employees engage in open warfare?"

"One with a sense of humor?" The beginning of a smile tipped up the corners of his expressive mouth. "By the way, do you have any idea why our mysterious owner chose you for the job?" Laying his arm across her shoulders, he guided her toward a door on the other side of the room. "I assumed the owner chose me because the Maguires have a reputable name in Galveston."

Amanda's breath escaped her in a small hiss at the unexpected touch of his arm. It had to be escaping steam, because she was definitely boiling on several levels. First off, she couldn't use her decorating skills if a man who was in love with lime green was constantly undermining her.

Secondly, Con was still summer heat lightning and distant thunder on her sensual horizon. If she spent too much time with him, she might be flattened by the storm. The collateral damage could be ugly. It would be hard to ignore the erotic connection she'd always felt when he was near. And here she'd thought she would outgrow Conleth Maguire. Silly her.

She needed her anger. It was her shield. With it she could do her job and return to New York untouched. He'd dented her shield a little with his explanation of what happened ten years ago. But she could get mad again. He was attempting to interfere with her job. Yes, Conleth Maguire was the one man she couldn't hook up with again. So she'd just stay mad at him.

"When Holgarth contacted my office in New York, he said my work had impressed the owner, and I had Galveston roots. He was big on the Galveston roots. Holgarth sweetened the pot by offering me an obscene amount to take the job and promising my work would be promoted in the national media. I'm still building my reputation, and I need all the exposure I can get." She tried to unobtrusively slip from under Con's arm, but it was a no-go. The weight and heat of him remained Super-Glued to her shoulders, a small reminder of the weight and heat of other parts of him. He'd be surprised to know how much she *did* remember about his body.

Con opened the door and led her to an elevator. "The castle has the prerequisite narrow winding stone steps, but I didn't think you wanted to experience all that authenticity right now." He waited for her to enter the elevator and then hit the button for the top floor of the tower.

When the elevator doors slid open, she burst out ahead of him and exhaled the breath she'd been holding all the way up. It was tough not to breathe for three hours. At least that's how long the ride had seemed crowded into a tiny space with Con and his army of sensual weapons. His pheromone attack had failed because she'd stopped breathing, but sexual awareness had squeezed her into a corner while superheated memories attacked her in waves.

Each floor of the castle's towers only had two rooms. Not much of a choice on this floor, Sleeping Princess or Brave Prince. Ugh. She was going to earn her money whipping this place into shape. Unlocking the Sleeping Princess door, she pushed it open and stepped inside. Behind her, she sensed Con waiting for her reaction.

She didn't disappoint. "Ack!" Bright pulsating pink and bleached-bones white. No wonder the princesses who stayed here slept so much.

Con moved over to the white canopy bed with the gauzy pink hangings. "The two rooms on this floor are the only ones left from the castle's previous incarnation. The owner hired Dad to do the renovations, and he's gutted all of the other rooms."

"I want to marry your dad." Weary, she looked for a chair. No chair. No way would she sit on the bed while Galveston's sexual magnet was looming over it. All he'd have to do is lean close enough to draw her into his magnetic field and she'd be stuck to his delicious body for the rest of the night.

Besides, sitting on a bed with Con in the room would

invite memories—his powerful body, bare and poised above her, her cries of . . . nope, didn't want to think of that. She sat down instead on the fuzzy white carpet. Slipping off her sandals, she stretched her legs out in front of her, wiggled her toes, and leaned back against the pink-striped wall.

Turning her head, she came face-to-face with Deimos's interested stare. "Where'd he come from?"

"He must've run up the stairs and slipped in when you opened the door." Con picked up her shoes and headed for what she assumed was the bathroom. He was silent for a moment, and all she heard was water running into the sink.

"Have you noticed anything strange about Deimos?" he asked from the bathroom.

She glanced into the cat's yellow eyes. Nope, no demon lights there. "Seems like just a cat to me. Okay, a clumsy cat and maybe a little obsessed with human companionship, but nothing else out of the ordinary. Why?"

"No reason." His tone said there *was* a reason, but he wasn't ready to talk about it. "What're your plans for the castle?"

"I want the place to have mellow old-world charm. Light-colored walls, dark wood furniture, and jewel-toned accessories. And of course authentic. It has to look authentic. I'll need some ancient-looking weaponry and tapestries with a medieval flavor to enhance the authentic feel." She narrowed her gaze on a white table where a sadly limp plant sat in a pale beam of sunlight. The table was pushed against the wall under an arrow slit that passed for a window. Poor droopy plant. It was a tiny island of green floating in a vast sea of putrid pink.

"I don't know about the walls." He came out of the bathroom holding her now clean sandals. "This is the Castle of Dark Dreams. Remember? I'm thinking dark walls, gargoyles, fetid dungeons, maybe even a murder hole. One of the castle guardians can stand on the battlements and pour boiling oil down on guests who try to sneak off without paying their bills."

She'd *never* been speechless. She was pretty sure that on the night she was born, when the doctor slapped her bottom, instead of crying she'd calmly pointed out the hospital's unfortunate color scheme.

She was speechless now. A slipstream of nightmare images trailed behind her careening imagination. Black walls. Velvet paintings accented in blood. Fake fur bedspreads. Lava lamps.

Ignoring her openmouthed horror, he sat on the floor facing her. He trapped her legs between his and then pulled her bare foot more snugly between his thighs as he prepared to put her sandals back on her feet. His gaze lifted to meet hers.

Amanda was still speechless, but for a completely different reason now. She remembered. They'd sat this way on the beach that night. She curled her toes reflexively, feeling again the cool wet sand beneath her feet, the even cooler breeze off the Gulf. But none of that chill could lower the heat they were generating or hold back the flames. Desire was the perfect combustible.

Swallowing hard, she tried to find her voice. She must have a deer-in-headlights expression. Who would've guessed she'd be ambushed by hot memories in the Sleeping Princess room?

Con's gaze darkened, and his lips parted slightly. He remembered, too. Of course, she didn't want him to remember anything that would interfere with their business relationship. *Uh-huh, and you're a pitiful liar.*

"We have unfinished business, sweet-heat." His voice was a husky murmur of erotic promise.

Amanda opened her mouth knowing there was a very real possibility nothing but a panicked squeak would emerge. What had happened to all that self-assurance she'd cultivated over the years? She mentally got down on her hands and knees searching for it. Here, backbone. Come to Mama. Nope, her backbone had left the building.

"The only business we have together is getting this castle ready for the public." Take that, Conleth Maguire.

His smile was slow, sensual, and said that no matter how good she'd been at handling everything else in her life, she'd never been any good at all when it came to handling him.

Handling him. Oops. Freudian slip. "Just put my damned shoes on so I can get up." Good. A healthy "damned" always made an assertive statement.

"No."

Checkmate. Now what? Wrestling him for her shoes lacked dignity, and she was all about dignity. Besides, initiating physical contact would just play into his hands. Literally.

Con watched her, seeing every one of her thoughts in her eyes. He laughed softly. "Come and get them, Mandy." And wondered at what point his mouth had parted company with his brain. But it wasn't his brain that was driving him now. It was a primitive part of him that bypassed thinking in favor of pure sensation, a part that had never forgotten sex with Amanda Harcourt.

For a moment, he thought she'd jerk her foot away, stand, and then start tacking up paint chips on the wall. She surprised him.

"I can make you give them back." Her smile held the remembrance of what they'd done ten years ago and how good it had been. "Don't make me resort to the foot torture."

"A threat? Intriguing." Con dropped his gaze as she moved her bare foot from his grasp and pressed it against his sex. He bit back a gasp as his body took notice of the pressure and reacted with positive growth.

Her eyes darkened, and he knew she felt him growing hard. This was probably not the best way to start a business relationship, but it was fourth and goal, and he wanted to score. That at least hadn't changed in ten years.

"I still remember that night, Mandy." He almost groaned as she pressed harder. "We were both naked, sitting like this. You put your foot against me and then . . ."

Her smile was wicked anticipation. "And then I did this."

She slowly rubbed her foot up and down against his erection, and when he figured he couldn't get any harder, she curled her bare toes into him. He closed his eyes and almost panted to keep from dragging her beneath him, having crazy sex with her, and then promising she could paint the walls any damned color she wanted.

With his last bit of self-control, he grasped her ankle and stilled her effort to visit death by foot massage on him. With his free hand, he handed her the sandals. "Your foot should be registered as a lethal weapon, lady."

"Yes, well, it sort of went off and did its own thing. I mean, I don't want you to think that foot was *me*. Those toes were out of control." She was all wide-eyed shock and disbelief. He wondered how long it had been since she'd let herself wander out of the neutral zone. "I'll bet my foot was kidnapped by aliens. They must've done horrible experiments on it, and then programmed it to make you a sexual minion who would help them conquer Earth." Lowering her gaze, she concentrated on putting her shoes back on. "I can't believe I just said that. I don't usually babble."

Con grimaced. Right now, his body was howling its rage. Sexual organs didn't take deprivation well. He'd leave his cock to work out its own painful destiny. He switched his brain back into reasoning mode. "Hey, we were both into the moment."

She stood. "It won't happen again."

"Sure." It would happen again.

Gingerly, she sat on the bed. "Did they prosecute the person who decorated this room?"

Amazing that for ten years he'd gone about his life like a normal man, not obsessing about any particular woman, just enjoying what came his way. He tried not to sweat anything. Life was too short. Mandy never could've understood his laid back attitude. It would've annoyed the hell out of her.

Thirty minutes with Mandy had destroyed that man. He wasn't quite sure what he was morphing into, or even if he'd like the final product, but he couldn't stop it, didn't *want* to stop it. "By the way, I have a new take on the Castle of Dark Dreams."

Mandy raised her eyes to the ceiling. "Thank you, God."

"I think we're talking dark as in sensual." He leaned back on his elbows, trying to bring visuals into focus.

"Sensual?" Mandy looked wary.

And well she should. "Yeah." He could see it now, deep red walls and erotic murals. He'd keep the murals as a surprise. She thought he was one-dimensional.

"I don't think the owner had that in mind. I'm not trying to restart our argument here, but the owner hired me to decorate the castle, and that includes wall colors. I've been trained for this. It's what I do. I'm willing to take your ideas into consideration, though." She smiled stiffly.

She was trying to appease the uncultured slob who'd just been hired to do the painting grunt work. Con knew he was probably being unfair, but he needed to be mad. If for no other reason than to convince his aroused body it hadn't wanted her anyway. But his body was too smart to buy that crap.

"Unless I missed something, I don't think the owner told us squat." Con shrugged. "So I'm going to interpret the Castle of Dark Dreams any way I want. Besides, Holgarth contracted my company to do the painting, and if I take my paint and go home, you have nothing." He regressed to a ten-year-old around this woman. Mandy bugged him. Her unswerving drive to be perfect had always driven him crazy. Of course, she'd also been a perfect lover. He was okay with *that*.

Con watched the horror return to her eyes. He had to admit he liked her playful sensual look better.

"You've spent a lifetime being the best at whatever you did—cheerleader, class president, top of your class. You were driven in high school, and then you went off to New York and I guess drove yourself some more. So you're a good designer, but don't give me that decorating diva act." What the hell? He'd never realized how mad he was with Amanda Harcourt. Where had all this anger come from? They'd had one night of incredible sex. She shouldn't be able to do this to him. "Give other people some credit for maybe having a few smarts." Shut your mouth, Maguire. You have to work with her. "Tell me something, Mandy. Does being the best at everything make you happy?" That was cold. And that last comment wasn't who he was. He was a live and let live kind of guy.

She looked stricken. "I'm not—"

Con held up his hand. "Look, I'm sorry." Rising, he raked his fingers through his hair. "How you live your life is your own business." He fixed his eyes on her toes as he walked toward her. Pale pink polish. Soft, feminine, and able to bring a grown man to his knees.

A sudden blur of motion made him look up just in time to see Deimos leap across the white table in a soaring trajectory aimed at the arrow slit's ledge. Mandy turned to follow Con's gaze.

Deimos's trajectory calculations were a little off, though, because the only part of him that hit the ledge was his chin. Tumbling back onto the table, he rolled off taking the limp plant with him. Con winced as the cat hit the floor and came up wearing the pot on his head like a battle trophy. Mandy would approve. It was a neutral pot. The hapless plant lay on the white carpet in a scatter of dirt.

Con could tell that Mandy was biting back laughter. "How about a chorus of 'Oops, I Did It Again?'"

Con shook his head. "I really believed cats always landed on their feet. Learn something new every day." He reached down to lift the pot off Deimos's head.

"Look, dumbass, I'm not used to handling four legs. Okay? I just wanted to get away from all that X-rated garbage you guys were projecting. You need to throw cold water on those mental images. Young and innocent eyes are watching here." Deimos sat down and used one spotted paw to scrape off a few mangled leaves from his head. *"I hate this job. I want real action, violence, destruction. You know, guy stuff."*

Con sucked in his breath as he stared down at the cat. The pot fell unnoticed to the floor. "Tell me you heard that, Mandy."

"Heard what?" Mandy frowned at the dirt. "Where's the vacuum?"

He didn't answer. The cat had spoken in his head. Again. Con wasn't imagining it this time. No blaming it on the heat. When he was a kid, he used to imagine he had magical powers like his supposed Druid ancestors. But this wasn't make-believe, and he wasn't a kid anymore. First he had to figure out if this was real or if he was going crazy. Who could he ask? Not Mandy. She already half thought he was nuts.

She turned to see why he hadn't answered, and sudden concern flooded her eyes. "You look terrible. You're gray and"—she put her palm on his forehead—"clammy. It's the heat. We need to get some liquids into—"

She never got a chance to finish her sentence, because Sparkle Stardust rushed into the room. Sparkle's face was red, and she was puffing. "Ran all the way up those damned stairs." She scanned the room. "Someone hurt Sweetie Pie. I felt her cry out to me."

Her? Con could've sworn Deimos was male. Mandy glanced at Con for inspiration, but he could only shrug. How could he concentrate on Sparkle when he was trying to come to terms with the bizarre fact that a cat was talking in his head?

Mandy's expression said he was a poor excuse for a hero. "Deimos is fine. It was . . ."

Sparkle swept by all of them, including Deimos, without a glance. She plunked herself on the floor beside the plant, scooped it up gently, and then held it cradled against her chest. "Who did this to you?"

If the blasted plant answered her, Con was gone.

"It was an accident. Deimos was trying to jump onto the ledge, and he misjudged the distance." Mandy's tone said she pretty much thought Sweetie Pie was too traumatized to get her facts straight, and why was everyone so bent out of shape?

Sparkle glanced at Deimos and cocked her head as though she was listening to something only she could hear. Con had a good idea what it was.

"Oh for crying out loud. Cut the whining. I guess I have to do everything myself." Sparkle stood and then picked up Sweetie Pie's pot. "I've got to get her back in her pot right away."

"Are you talking to me?" Mandy looked completely confused.

"Hmm?" Sparkle looked at Mandy as if she'd just seen her. "No, I'm talking to Deimos." She shifted her attention to Con. "I hope you guys will be getting it on soon."

Con stared at Sparkle, Deimos, and Sweetie Pie. This was some serious weirdness. "Is this place cursed?"

Sparkle smiled, a sly calculating lift of her lips. "I'm not asking for myself, hot bod. I'm asking for Sweetie Pie."

"Ah, everything is clear now." Mandy looked amused. "You want Con and *Sweetie Pie* to hook up."

Sparkle cast Mandy a slitty-eyed glare. "Is this where I'm supposed to laugh?"

Mandy had the sense to shut up.

"Sweetie Pie's well-being is in your hands . . ." Sparkle paused to consider her words. "Or other body parts. According to Holgarth, the owner wants you guys to take care of the plants. I was just keeping an eye on them until you got here." She carefully set Sweetie Pie in her dirtless pot.

"Here's the fun part. The owner enjoys studying plant behavior. Experiments have shown plants react to the things humans do and say. Plants seem to be healthiest in places with a lot of sexual activity." Sparkle smiled a wicked smile. "So I guess we'll all know how things are going by how perky Sweetie Pie and her siblings are."

Satisfied with her bombshell, Sparkle carried Sweetie Pie to the door and then paused. "I'll bring her back once I've replaced her soil."

As Sparkle left the room, Deimos trailed after her. He glanced at Con before disappearing. *"I hope you're not buying that. Umm, but if you do decide to help old Sweetie Pie get perky again, let me know your schedule so I can be far, far away."*

After they were gone, Mandy closed the door and leaned her back against it. "Tell me that woman didn't say we had to have sex so the plants would stay healthy."

"That's what she said." Now why hadn't he ever thought of that for a school science fair project? He shook his head to clear it. Forget the plants, he had more important things to think about.

"And what's with Deimos? You and Sparkle were acting strange around him." She was talking to him, but her gaze was riveted on the small pile of dirt.

Ha! She thought a pile of dirt was her biggest worry. "Deimos was talking to us." Mandy wouldn't believe him, but he wanted to see her expression anyway.

"Uh-huh." She never took her eyes off the dirt. "I need a vacuum cleaner."

"There's one in my room."

Long pregnant pause. "And that would be where?"

"Across the hall."

A longer, more pregnant pause. "Uh-huh. So you're the Brave Prince."

"I slay what dragons I must for my queen."

"You only live a block away."

He shrugged. "It's in my contract."

She shifted her attention from the dirt to his face. She sighed. "I knew I should've asked for more money."

CHAPTER ◆ THREE

Amanda should've known it wouldn't last. A week of uneasy peace was more than she'd expected. Con and his men had worked outside all week painting the keep white to make it look as though the stones had been lime-washed.

She knew this because each day she spent her lunch hour in recreational babe-watching. Con might own the company, but he worked right alongside his men—shirtless, muscles rippling, skin gleaming with sweat. Hot visuals equaled fever. After each lunch hour, she jacked up the air to Arctic level.

She hadn't left the castle much except when she drove into Houston to buy furnishings, rugs, and accessories that would put her unique signature on the castle. They hadn't been together, ergo no fighting. The separation hadn't done a thing to ease the sexual tension, though. Like the Gulf tides, it rose and fell with regularity, although each day high tide lasted a little longer.

Shutting down her notebook, she stared at the blank wall of the great hall. A soon to be cream wall. She didn't think Con was a cream kind of guy. Amanda sighed. He'd fight her. And even if she won, she'd lose, because she'd bet he believed in payback.

Which made her think about this morning. No more peaceful coexistence. She'd peeked outside and watched as he took up where he'd left off a week ago. Red trim. Rushing outside, she'd ordered him to cease and desist. Words were spoken, then shouted. Without warning, he'd grown quiet and said he'd paint the damned trim white. *Yes.* She'd won, she'd won. She maintained her dignity until she was safely back in the castle. Then she allowed herself a mini victory dance. Only afterward did she pause to wonder why he'd given in so easily. Amanda knew enough about Conleth Maguire to figure he was probably planning to run right around her defensive line into the end zone.

The object of her worry swung wide the castle doors and strode into the great hall bringing the smell of fresh paint with him. Wet paint was a sexy smell.

"Done for the day?" Duh, yes. Like you haven't timed down to the second what time he quits each day?

Con nodded. "I'm heading up to my room so I can take a shower." He glanced at her. "You have a line between your eyes. Doing some deep thinking?"

It never occurred to her to tell the truth. She wasn't sure what that said about the deteriorating state of her character. "Sweetie Pie is still droopy. I tried talking dirty to her. She perked up a little, but when she realized I wasn't following up my talk with action, she went back to being sad. Any ideas?"

His laugh was incredulous. "Is this a trick question? What do you *think* my idea is?"

"Sex. Right. Forget I asked." She couldn't make love with Con, because he was the one man who might be able to compete with her career. She didn't want to be conflicted. Amanda would just let Sweetie Pie wilt and die. Then she'd deliver the dead body to Holgarth with appropriate regrets. "Oh, you can start painting the great hall as soon as you get the paint."

He stilled. A dangerous quiet that spoke of silent predators crouched in jungle shadows.

"Meow."

Hmm. As jungle predators went, that was pretty weak. Wait. That wasn't Con, it was . . . Amanda glanced down. Deimos stared up. He crouched. She put a protective arm across her notebook. He leaped. She closed her eyes as he slid across the small table and fell off the other end. At least he hadn't taken her notebook with him.

"What color, Mandy?" Now that was how a true jungle cat should sound, all husky and threatening.

Mandy watched as Deimos picked himself up, sat down to wash his face, and then casually padded away as if he'd never wanted to be on the dumb table anyway.

"Color?" Con shifted closer.

He was down to one-word questions. Not a good

sign. Amanda figured she'd better answer before he abandoned words altogether and resorted to action. Even though the threat of action kind of turned her on, action probably involved touching. And right now her sexual tension tide was almost at flood stage. No, touching would not be a good thing.

"Cream."

"Last time I looked, this was the Castle of Dark Dreams, not a dessert." Anger simmered and bubbled just below the surface of his self-control. "This room needs rich sensual colors. Had any dark dreams lately, sweet-heat? I bet they weren't decorated in cream."

Okay, no more Ms. Congeniality. "Why do you care? Most men wouldn't give a damn what color I painted this room." She couldn't wait for his answer, so she answered herself. "I'll tell you why. It's because I chose cream. You would've hated any color I chose. What's your freaking problem, Maguire?" Wow, she'd scared herself. She sounded like the seventeen-year-old girl who'd lusted after Con Maguire. The one who'd liked clingy purple tops, heated arguments, and loud laughter. But it felt good on a strictly emotional level.

His mood seemed to improve in direct proportion to her anger. "I think we need to discuss this. Go out and check to make sure I didn't paint any of your trim red, because you know that's what you want to do. Then come up to my room and we'll . . . consult." His grin was wide, taunting, and sexy as hell.

"You bet. I'll do just that." Huffing and puffing, she

slammed out of the castle, her bad temper propelling her to the gate where she'd first seen him painting.

At first glance, the castle trim looked white. She let some of her anger go. Everything seemed to be . . . no, everything wasn't okay. She moved closer to the gate. Lime green snakes! Scattered along the length of the trim were small lime green snakes. Ohmigod. They all had long lashes, blue eyes, and small blue butterflies on their tails.

She'd kill him. She didn't care if they were whimsical little snakes. She didn't stop to think about the talent that created them. All she cared about was the blue butterflies on their tails. Who gave him the right to expose her butterfly in a public forum? It felt like she'd pulled down her pants and mooned the world.

She grabbed her cell phone from her skirt's pocket and called Holgarth. Now that she thought about it, how did Holgarth get off living somewhere else? She'd include Holgarth in her roaring bad mood.

"Holgarth, here. I assume the castle is in flames or being attacked by barbarian hordes, because I truly can't think of any other reasons that would warrant you disturbing me at home, Ms. Harcourt." He either had caller ID or had recognized her heavy breathing.

"Conleth Maguire painted snakes on the trim around the gate. Who's the designer here? If you want me to do a good job, then I damn well better have some authority. I want to talk to the owner." Blue *butterflies* on their tails.

"Snakes? How enterprising of him. The owner values creativity." Holgarth took snide and snotty to a whole new level. "The owner wishes not to be disturbed, as do I, Ms. Harcourt. You will simply have to deal with Mr. Maguire yourself. I'm sure he'll soon recognize your superior skills."

Holgarth had mastered the big three—snide, snotty, and sarcastic. What a guy.

"It amazes me, Holgarth, that the owner is paying me a fortune to professionally decorate this place, and yet doesn't give a flip if someone with no professional training at all inflicts his taste on the castle. Go figure." She disconnected and wished she'd called from the phone in her room so she could've slammed the receiver down. If she were a true professional, she'd pack her bags right now and go back to New York. But she intended to stay, and she wasn't ready to question why.

Shoving the phone into her pocket, she walked back into the castle. She climbed the stairs to give herself a chance to cool down. No use going ballistic over the exterior. She needed to concentrate her efforts on the interior. Besides, arguments weren't won by incoherent babbling. When she reached his room, she knocked. No answer. Well, he'd invited her to his room. She twisted the knob. Unlocked. Without a twinge of guilt, she opened the door and stepped inside.

The sound of running water reached her. He was still in the shower. She'd give a shout just so he couldn't accuse her of sneaking. "I'm here."

"I'll be out in a minute." He sounded suspiciously cheerful.

She'd make sure that didn't last long. How could he plaster a symbol of their night together all over the trim where the whole world could see? She should be frothing at the mouth over the green snakes, but the snakes were merely blips on her radar compared to those little butterflies. Where's your sense of humor, Harcourt? Her humor didn't extend to the butterfly on her behind.

Calm down. He only wins if you react. She did some deep breathing and in a few minutes felt almost tranquil.

The sound of running water stopped, and visuals of something more immediate replaced the hated blue butterflies. He'd probably stepped out of the shower, all bare and wet gleaming male. He'd reach for a towel.

She skipped right past images of him toweling his hair dry and rubbing the cloth over his yummy chest. She pulled up images from ten years ago, made age adjustments, and found them excellent. He'd run the towel over his stomach and then his gorgeous ass.

Freeze-frame. The guys she'd known in New York had firm, muscular, or rounded butts, but Conleth Maguire was the only man she'd ever elevated to "gorgeous ass" status. This was not a good thing. She'd wanted to come back to Galveston, look at it through her grown-up eyes, and proclaim that everything was better in New York, including asses. There was still hope, though. She hadn't seen Con's bare buns lately. Maybe they had lost some of their star quality over the years. She could only hope.

Okay, moving onward with her visuals of the Body-Maguire. Next, he'd reach between his legs, cup his . . .

Where was the thermostat? He must keep this place set at ninety degrees. For the first time, she looked around the room. Amanda blinked, and her sexy mental images disappeared. She hated when that happened. But she couldn't ignore bad taste.

Blue. Everything in the room was pale blue. Ugh, ugh, ugh. She finally located the thermostat. Hmm, seventy degrees. Must be wrong. She pushed it a few degrees lower, then took a closer look at the room.

There on the night table beside his bed sat a plant that was almost identical to Sweetie Pie. Except this plant was healthy, happy, and, dare she say it, perky. "Where'd you get this plant? It looks really . . . green."

"Jessica? She belongs to the owner." He turned on the hair dryer.

Why did Jessica look so happy? Amanda got all slitty-eyed thinking about how he might've kept Jessica entertained.

He turned off the dryer. "I can hear you thinking, Mandy. No, I didn't have crazy sex every night this week to keep the plant happy."

She could hear him coming out of the bathroom. "Then why does Jessica look so great? Did you slip her some plant food? How many times did you water her?" She turned toward the bathroom door.

And watched Con walk out with only a towel wrapped around his waist. The room immediately overflowed with perkiness. "Whoa, unfair advantage. Jessica is a she, and you're renewing her root system with the sight of all that bare skin."

During her years in New York, she'd had brief romances with a few men. They'd all shared her vision and been cool, calculating, calm men. Insight—had she subconsciously chosen men who were the exact opposite of Con? But they all faded to the same shade of blue as this room in comparison to Conleth Maguire. He was deep pulsating red. Her mental images hadn't done him justice.

He shrugged. "Sorry. I'm not going to dress in the closet for a plant." Lifting his gaze to hers, he smiled. A slow slide of heat. "Or you."

Amanda could feel the artificial layers of her New York self peeling off to reveal the real woman beneath. Desperately, she tried to pull them back on, but they didn't quite fit anymore. The scary part? Underneath the layers was someone she recognized from a long time ago. And there was nothing neutral about *her*.

She was a woman who was heating up just fine at the sight of a beautifully sculpted male body. A woman who could get down and dirty with a lean mean loving machine. A woman who'd scream her joy as she climaxed, and trace a black rose tattoo with her tongue. Sheesh, she was seventeen again.

He must've seen something in her eyes, because his smile turned predatory. "Have a seat." He gestured toward a blue chair. "I'll sit on the bed, and you can tell me all about why you think the walls in the great hall should be cream."

Amanda perched on the edge of the chair while he settled himself on the bed. Settled? Ha. Displayed would be a better word. As he sat cross-legged, his towel rode up so high that only shadows kept both Jessica and her from bursting into bloom.

She needed to get to the point of their conversation before she forgot what it was. A calm discussion about cream walls first. Then lots of shouting and arm waving about blue butterflies.

"I assume you're going to use your extensive knowledge of interior design to explain why the walls should be bloody red instead of cream." Okay, sarcasm would only beget more sarcasm. "Cream is a quiet color that doesn't have the sterile feel of white. It lets the warmth of wood, and the colors of furniture, paintings, and accessories come forward. Cream is always quietly powerful without fighting for supremacy."

"Wow, I'm impressed." He studied her a little too long and made her a little too uneasy.

"Well, what do you think?"

"I think a rich red would express what this castle is all about. Think, Mandy. We associate red with some of our deepest emotions—anger, passion, hate, and love. The Castle of Dark Dreams should reflect those emotions."

He had a surprising grasp of color, but then he'd taken art classes in high school. It didn't matter what he thought, though, Con's red-wall idea was going down. This wasn't about the castle at all. It was a defining of who they were.

His sudden smile was impossibly sweet and incredibly insincere. "Haven't you figured out by now that I didn't ask you to my room to talk about walls?"

Yes! That truth was from the sluts who lived in her basement. "I think the walls should be our *only* topic." That was from her penthouse dwellers who had a close working relationship with her brain.

"Later." A lot later. He supported his argument for later by leaning back slightly so that his towel slid even higher.

Sure, using his body was cheap, but after a week of hard-ons thinking about Mandy in his bed or any other place he could get her naked, he didn't give a damn.

She stared at his towel with wide-eyed alarm, and something else. Maybe it was wishful thinking, but he'd swear he saw hunger in her gaze. She'd better say something soon, because he was fast outgrowing his towel.

"Don't move. I'll be back in a few minutes." Mandy almost ran to the door and was gone. She'd been in such a hurry she didn't even close it behind her.

Well, hell. What was that about? Before he had time to think about closing the door, Darth Destroyer padded into the room. Con had avoided the cat for most of the week, because he was still way into denial. But now that he was faced with Deimos, Con had to find out once and for all if he needed a shrink.

"How'd you get into the castle, pal? I locked all the doors." He wasn't big on praying, but Con was praying right now for a simple meow.

"Trade secret. How's the sex thing going? Are you two gonna hook up?" Deimos clawed his way up the

bedspread and then sat facing Con. *"Still can't jump. The four legs don't want to work together. So let's talk sex. When're you gonna do it? Where're you gonna do it? Why haven't you done it yet? I need details, man."*

Sheer willpower kept Con on the bed. "Who are you? *What* are you?" He braced his hands on his knees to keep them from shaking.

Deimos cocked his head to study Con. *"Sorry about scaring you, but Sparkle said the cat form was best for spying. That first time, when I ended up wearing the paint, I didn't mean to talk to you. It just happened. You must have some old magic in your past, or you wouldn't have heard me."* He stretched out and made himself comfortable. *"Maguire. Irish, right? Any Druids in your past?"*

Con nodded. He gripped his knees so tightly his knuckles turned white. "Who *are* you?"

Deimos eyed Jessica with interest. *"If Sparkle finds out I'm telling you this, she'll kick me off the job. But she's already pissed, so what the hell."* He yawned. *"We're both cosmic troublemakers, supernatural beings who get off on causing trouble. Sort of the badasses of the universe."*

Con swallowed hard. This was not happening.

"It's happening. Believe it. My job is to make sure you copulate, fornicate, conjugate . . . all those 'ate' words. So let's talk about what a woman wants." The expression on Deimos's furry face said he wasn't quite sure what a woman wanted, but he'd give it his best shot.

"You should get naked first. Wait until I leave, though. I facilitate, but I don't rubberneck results."

"You can read my mind." He'd spent his childhood listening to Dad tell tales of magical happenings in Ireland. Con could almost accept paranormal events there. Ireland had a reputation for fairies, banshees, and haunted castles. But Galveston, Texas?

He had a choice. Either accept what was right in his face or run screaming from the room. Since he was pretty sure he wasn't crazy, Con had to believe Deimos was being straight with him. "I can take care of my own sex life. Why does Sparkle care about us anyway?"

"She specializes in creating sexual chaos by bringing together people who don't much like each other. She gets off on emotional turmoil. I have special talents in this area, so Sparkle is mentoring me." Deimos stood and moved closer to Jessica.

Con had real doubts about Deimos's talent level. "I don't get it. I like Mandy." His body affirmed he did indeed like her.

Deimos glared at him before edging even nearer to Jessica. *"My talent level's top-notch. But this isn't about me. It's about you hanging on to your mad because she went off and got a life of her own. Get over it, Maguire. Have sex with her. You know that's what you want to do."* He narrowed his eyes to sneaky slits. *"Either the earth will move, or it won't. What's to lose?"*

Anger pushed away Con's fear. Deimos must've been

reading his mind since the first time they met. "Stay out of my mind."

"Or else you'll do what?" Deimos oozed obnoxious self-confidence.

Con thought about Sparkle. She'd deliver some serious butt kicking. "I'll tell Sparkle you can't even stay in the room to make sure the job's done right."

Deimos hissed at him. *"Okay, okay, I'll stay out. But you might need me soon."* He was so close to Jessica now that his nose was almost touching a leaf.

"Don't hold your breath." Con wanted the cat gone so he could pull himself together before Mandy came back. *If* she came back.

"Hey, don't insult the cat with inside info. Remember, I'm the only one who can read your woman's mind for you." Deimos touched one of the plant's leaves with his tongue. *"Turns me on like catnip. Jessica's one hot babe. Think I have a chance?"*

"Get. Out. Of. Here." He wondered how ticked Sparkle would be if he laid some serious damage on her precious apprentice.

"Sure. Sure. Let me know what happens tonight so I can pass it on to Sparkle and make believe it was a live report." Scrambling from the bed, Deimos fled the room.

Con drew in a deep calming breath. He had to push what had just happened to the back of his mind until he could deal with it. But Deimos had a point. Con had never expected Mandy to come back to Galveston, and when she did, his first impulse was anger. Why the anger? Who knew? But when had anger kept him from wanting Amanda Harcourt? Never.

Con stopped thinking as Mandy returned to the room. She had Sweetie Pie in her hand. Walking around his bed, she set Sweetie Pie next to Jessica. "I figure a few days with you will give new meaning to her life."

"We could give new meaning to her life a lot faster than that." Con was through being subtle. He wanted to lay her down on his bed, slide his fingers though her hair, and cover her mouth with his while her body came alive beneath him. He'd touch every warm secret spot on her body with his mouth, and then bury himself in her, creating a new memory to take the place of the one from ten years ago.

She saw the intent in his eyes, and the part of her that had worked damn hard for ten years to earn her BA in mature decisions demanded she leave. Now.

He unwound from his cross-legged position and then swung his feet to the floor. His towel slipped a little lower on his hips.

Her mature self pointed out that taking pleasure with Conleth Maguire would be a really poor business decision. If he thought he could override her color choices now, what would happen once they made love? She'd end up with purple walls with neon orange smiley faces on them.

Con stood and walked toward her, each stride focusing her attention on the towel's precarious position.

Each stride showcasing the beauty of powerful muscles beneath smooth, supple skin.

Her mature self, still calm and firmly in control, assured her she'd walked away from men with beautiful bodies before. Beautiful bodies didn't mean a thing if there was a troll inside.

He stopped in front of her. Six feet plus of power, muscle, and the mysterious ability to roll back time. She expected to be Zit Central at any moment.

They should talk. Ten years ago they'd made spectacular love on that beach. But when it was over, it was over. That was at the root of her anxiety now. If it was all about sex, she didn't want any part of it. Been there, done that ten years ago. Fine, so she wanted something deeper, more meaningful, right? Well, no. Deeper and more meaningful might tempt her to stay in Galveston. What *did* she want? That depended on which body system was answering. Right now there was a catfight heating up between her brain and the sluts in her basement.

"We should talk." Her mature self applauded.

Leaning down, he touched her throat with his mouth. Her heart beat hard and fast beneath his lips. He smelled like Irish Spring and toothpaste. Her list was growing. Paint, Irish Spring, and toothpaste smelled sexy.

"No." The warmth of the one word against her skin brought a shuddering response that surprised her.

"Why not?" She knew why not, but the question gave her a moment to search for guidance from her know-it-all mature self. Instant gratification or deep and meaningful? What to do? Okay, soul searching done. Call her shallow, but his totally delicious body was as deep and meaningful as she wanted to get right now.

"Because I've had a hard-on all week imagining you naked in this bed. A man can't paint in high places with a hard-on. I think there's some kind of local ordinance against it." He moved his mouth to the sensitive skin below her ear and traced lazy circles with his tongue.

Mistake, mistake, mistake! Amanda sighed. Her mature self may as well shut up. It was a big fat loser. She was going to ignore her common sense and ten years of accumulated lessons learned. She'd go with what she wanted just because she wanted it. Her desire for Con went beyond the hurt feelings of a seventeen-year-old, beyond her fear of any complication that would interfere with her New York career. If New York couldn't stand up to one night with Con, then she needed to find out now.

"We can't have you turning into an outlaw." Leaning forward, she slid her tongue across one of his nipples. He sucked in his breath. "Of course, there's something really sexy about an outlaw with a hard-on."

His soft laughter spurred her on.

"Just call me the Lone Arranger. I can arrange your furniture or a hot night of sex." She laid both palms flat against his chest. "Kinky or otherwise." His skin was still damp from his shower, and his nipples pressed into her palms. The pressure registered as an anticipatory clenching low in her belly. "I'm here to save you from a life of crime, restore Sweetie Pie to perkiness, and find out if you're still as spectacular as I remember." She

reached between them with one hand and yanked his
towel from his hips. As she let the towel drop to the
floor, she glanced down. "Everything does grow bigger
in Texas."

"Well, hell." His voice was husky with need and more
than a little surprise. "Kinky or otherwise? I like it. I
knew my wicked woman was hiding in there somewhere.
Looks like Ms. Neutral has shifted into first gear."

She leaned into him, feeling the length of his bare
body pressed against her. It had been so long, and she
was so eager. "Wrong, oh great and magical painter of
snakes. It's been a lot of years since I've traveled the
open road"—she slid her hands over his arms, his torso,
and his thighs to indicate the road she had in mind—
"and I'm shifting right through to fifth gear."

His answer was to put his hands on her shoulders and
lower his head to cover her mouth with his. She kept her
lips closed so he'd understand the walls might be
breached, but she wasn't flinging the gate open for him.
Not right away, anyway.

Walls. Uh-uh, didn't want to think of walls, or her
job, or the snakes now. She wanted to immerse herself
in Conleth Maguire and maybe recapture a little of what
she'd left behind ten years ago.

He traced her lower lip with his tongue and then gently nipped it. Okay, fifteen seconds was long enough to
make her point. Time to fling the gates open. She parted
her lips and met his tongue with an eagerness that told
her she'd wanted this for longer than she realized.

With a low moan of joy, she savored the taste of

toothpaste and the essence of what had always made him an irresistible temptation to her. The pressure of his lips increased, signaling his escalating excitement.

He dropped his hands from her shoulders and stepped away, his breathing ragged in the quiet room. "We need to take our time, sweet-heat. Ten years ago, we ripped each other's clothes off, fell on the sand, and went crazy. This time we should savor it."

"Right. We're adults now. We'll walk to the bed, I'll calmly undress—"

"No way. *I'll* calmly undress you."

From the length, breadth, and stiffness of his erection, Amanda doubted his ability to do anything calmly. She, on the other hand, had spent ten years training in the "calm" arena.

She reached for a button on her blouse with shaking fingers. Calm. She took a step toward the bed. Calm. She slid her gaze up Con's beautiful male body and thought about raking her fingers through his dark hair. Calm. She met his gaze.

He was heat, flame, and she was a damned moth. If she singed her wings, so be it. "What the hell, I can't wait." She pulled her blouse from her skirt and fumbled with the buttons.

Con joined her in a tangle of fingers and muffled curses. She was never quite sure who was responsible, but her blouse fell to the rug in a flurry of flying buttons. She kicked off her sandals, shimmied out of her skirt, and wrestled with Con for the privilege of ripping off her bra and panties.

As soon as he retrieved his foil package from the night table, she pulled him down with her onto the bed chanting her mantra of the moment, "Quickquickquick."

He eased her onto her back. She spread her legs so he could kneel between them. Since they were doing the mature love scene, she'd allow for about, say, three minutes of foreplay. Hey, she didn't want to rush things.

She pulled his head down to her breasts. It'd been a lot of years. Maybe he'd forgotten where they were. But when he slid his tongue across one nipple and then nipped it, she immediately forgot where *she* was. He closed his lips around her nipple, and the triple assault of heat, tongue, and pressure narrowed her world to only one sense: touch.

Burying her fingers in his hair, she let the silky strands slide through them. Her nipples were sensitive points of pleasure-pain, and she arched her back just in case he was thinking of abandoning them.

He did. The rat. With complete unconcern for her three-minute foreplay time limit, he kissed a searing path over her stomach and then her inner thighs. She knew where he was headed, and she'd explode if he touched her *there* with his mouth.

Grasping his shoulders, she rolled, and he rolled with her . . . over the edge of the bed and onto the floor. They almost took Sweetie Pie and Jessica with them. When she finally managed to disentangle herself from the bed-spread, wonder of wonders, she was straddling him. The view was to die for. A smooth, unbroken expanse of fine Texas male. All of his muscles were clearly delineated as he tightened them in an effort to last through those endless three minutes. Poor baby. He wouldn't have to suffer much longer.

"Geez, Maguire. I'd forgotten all of this." She illustrated all of this by splaying her fingers across his incredible abs. She hadn't really forgotten, but she sure didn't want him to think she'd obsessed over his body.

"Maybe you should feel around to see what else you remember." His voice sounded strained.

As she gazed into his hazel eyes gleaming with carnal knowledge and erotic promises, Mandy swore she saw the shadow of his Druid ancestor. Because Con was definitely magic.

Reaching between his legs, she walked her fingertips over his balls, and finished off by gliding her fingers over the rigid length of him. Amazing how emotion could feed off the senses. His erection was strength sheathed in warm satin, and just touching it made her want to cry. No, that was wrong. A body part couldn't make her cry, but the total wonderful package that was Conleth Maguire certainly could do the job.

He clasped her wrist. "Stop. I can't take anymore."

Good. Three minutes up. Her body clenched around the anticipation of an enormous orgasm, a Texas-sized orgasm. Wow, it felt good to be home. Something about that thought bothered her, but she couldn't think coherently enough to figure it out.

She needed him deep inside her. Now. Moving her body over his hips, she lowered herself until the head of his erection nudged between her spread legs. Oh, yesss.

"Wait." The voice of the devil. "I need something."

Like her undying curse? While she searched for one evil enough for the occasion, he reached up and felt around on the bed until he found the foil package. He seemed to rip it open in slow motion. *Arrgh.* It took him a good hour to put it on.

Finally finished, he lifted her back into position. "Ride me hard, sweet-heat. We have a lot of pleasure to catch up on."

Closing her eyes, she savored her tactile impressions. The weight of his hands on her thighs, the pressure of his cock pushing into her, spreading her, tempting her to let go. No way could she lower herself slowly onto that spectacular male display. She wanted all of him at once.

With a cry of triumph, she drove down on him, feeling him slide smoothly into her, filling her. She stilled, holding onto the sensation of complete connection, and then she began to move. Raising herself and then pushing down, she renewed over and over her sense of fullness. He picked up the rhythm, driving into her deeper and harder with each thrust.

Suddenly, all of her senses kicked back in. She moaned as he rolled her nipples between his fingers and the frenzy of their thrusts gained momentum. His breathing was a harsh rasp, and his scent of clean male and sexual excitement fueled her drive to orgasm. Frantic for more contact, she leaned forward and clamped her teeth in his shoulder to keep from screaming as he drove into her so hard she knew she'd shatter into a million shards if she didn't somehow anchor herself.

Her orgasm caught her, flung her high, and then rolled over her in wave after wave of unspeakable pleasure. She felt Con stiffen, straining toward that last moment before climax, and then he shouted as it took him.

As her spasms slowly faded, Mandy released Con's shoulder. What an incredible trip. "That was unbelievable."

"Unbelievable." Con was still breathing hard. He turned his head to look at his shoulder. "There're teeth marks."

She offered him a satiated smile. "Did I ever tell you about my vampire ancestors? Hot sex brings out my need to feed."

He returned her smile, but there was an emotion she didn't recognize in his eyes. "It was worth the bite. It couldn't have been this great ten years ago. Ten years ago I was a lot weaker. This kind of sex would've killed me."

When they'd gathered enough energy, they moved from the floor back to the bed. Con glanced at his clock. "That took us all of ten minutes."

Mandy smiled. "That long? I'm glad we've matured."

CHAPTER ◆ FOUR

"I'm driving into Houston tomorrow to buy wall sconces. Maybe I'll cruise on over to the Galleria and scope out red dresses." Mandy turned on her side to face him. "You've put me in a red-dress mood."

He tried not to look too hopeful. "How about red walls? Are you up for Ming Red? The owner of an old Victorian house in town had me paint—"

She scowled. "Don't push it, Maguire."

He tried to whip himself into a berserker frenzy over wall colors. It didn't work. He'd expended all his energy on the sexual frenzy of a few minutes ago. "So what turned you into a cream kind of woman? In high school—"

She reached over to lay her finger across his lips. "Don't say it. My color schemes were loud and proud of it. Those were my wicked woman days."

"I liked her. A lot." Con never missed an opportunity when it was pressed against his lips. He clasped her wrist and then closed his lips around her finger while he held her gaze. Slowly, thoroughly, he twirled his tongue around her finger, implying that his mouth was capable of so much more than what she'd already experienced.

Her eyes darkened, heated. Message received. He released her finger.

Mandy looked away before speaking. "I didn't inherit my preference for cream. Mom and Dad are earth-tone advocates." She glanced back at him and grinned. "By the way, they're loving retirement in Arizona. Anyway, you know I'm an only child, and they had me late in life. Something about that combination must've turned me into the overachiever from hell. They never put pressure on me, but I sure put it on myself. I had to be the best in everything, and if I had to change into something totally not me in order to be the best, I did it."

Con propped himself up on one elbow to study her. "Was it worth it?"

Her gaze turned distant, and he knew she was seeing the teen she'd been. "I sure thought so at the time."

"How do you feel about it now?" He held his breath, afraid she'd change the subject. They'd shared lust and a few laughs during her senior year, but they hadn't shared anything real of themselves.

Mandy rolled over onto her back and stared at the blue ceiling. "I don't know. All those things: the straight A's, the cheerleading, the student council—while I made sure I was just bad enough so no one would think I was geeky—made me feel accepted. Acceptance was my holy grail." She reached between them and clasped his hand. He squeezed it. "Who knows why certain things obsess us. It's the now thing to blame every kink in our psyches on our parents, but Mom and Dad were innocent."

He laughed. "I must've driven you crazy. I was so laid back I was unconscious. My grades were okay, but I didn't burn a lot of brain cells during high school. Just enough to get by. Football was a natural for me, so I did it. If I'd had to work hard to be good, I would've blown it off."

She didn't laugh. "I was jealous. You didn't let anything get to you. Life just flowed around you."

Now she'd really shocked him. "And here I thought my attitude frustrated the hell out of you."

She remained quiet so long he thought she wouldn't answer. "Did you ever go to art school?"

Con nodded. "I worked for Dad during the day and went to U of H at night. Since graduating, I've gotten good enough to sell some of my paintings. I'll probably always keep my day job, though, because I like the physical labor. It balances the other half of my life." Here goes the big question. "Why're you telling me everything now?"

Mandy turned her head to look at him. "Because we didn't talk ten years ago. Maybe if we had, things would've been different."

Left unsaid, but understood, was that maybe she wished things had worked out between them. His instant rush of emotion left him wary.

He sensed she'd done enough soul baring for one night. Con wouldn't press her for more. "We were kids, and kids are dumb."

"Oh, I almost forgot, you asked about the 'cream' me. It's my decorating persona, and I've done well with it. When I got to New York, I researched my target customer base, decided on an image that would get a positive response from them, and became that image. It worked in high school, and it's worked in my business. And yes, sometimes I even paint walls bright colors, but not these walls. I still think they should be cream." She frowned.

For a moment, he thought she was aiming her frown at him, until he realized she was looking over his shoulder. "What?"

"Umm, Sweetie Pie looks energized. Please tell me I'm wrong. I want her to be limp and droopy, because I really don't want to believe she got off on our lovemaking." Mandy sat up to get a better view of the plants.

Con didn't give a damn about Sweetie Pie. Mandy took his breath away. He'd accepted she was beautiful in a cool elegant way, but this . . . She was gorgeous in a way he hadn't seen before. Her cheeks were still flushed from sex, her lips swollen from his kisses, and her eyes soft with lazy sensual fulfillment. And her hair was tousled. He wanted to lean forward, touch that soft mouth with his lips, and bury his fingers in the silky strands of blond hair.

"Con, look at Sweetie Pie." She wasn't going to give it up.

Silently wishing an attack of aphids on the hapless Sweetie Pie, he turned over to look. Geez, he needed out of this place. Everything that happened here was creepy, and he didn't have a high tolerance for creepiness. Sweetie Pie looked like the Plant Fairy had given her an adrenaline shot. And Jessica looked like she'd put out a batch of new leaves. No way would he make love again in front of these leafy voyeurs. Listen to yourself. You're nuts.

"Simple explanation." He tried for casual, but it didn't quite come off. "All our heavy breathing put a lot more carbon dioxide into the air. Sweetie Pie and Jessica are loving it."

Mandy's expression said that was a bunch of crap. He thought so, too.

"Maybe I should go back to my—"

"No." Now that he had Mandy in his bed, he was revved for a hot night of love. Not in front of the plants, though. The total stupidity of that thought made him wince. Sparkle had said the plants fed off their energy. They couldn't *see*. Still . . . The solution seemed simple. He'd turn off the lights. For just a moment, though, he wondered about their night vision. This place is turning you into a wacko, Maguire. "Stay here tonight."

She nodded. "We can talk some more about cream walls. And I haven't even gotten started on blue butterflies. But first I need a shower." She swung her legs to the floor, stood, and then wiggled her fantastic little behind all the way to the bathroom. She'd kill him, but he'd die a happy man.

As soon as he heard the water running, he got up and went to the door. Con figured someone would be waiting for him on the other side. Flinging open the door, he looked down. Yep, mini-snoop was waiting.

"Geez, man. You're naked. Do something about it. You don't come to the door like that. Nuns could be collecting for charity. Girl Scouts could be selling cookies." Deimos kept his gaze focused somewhere over Con's left shoulder.

"Give me a break, Deimos." But he went back into the room, picked up his discarded towel, and wrapped it around his waist. Then he returned to the door. "How old are you anyway?"

"Four. Sparkle's thousands of years old, that's why none of this shit bothers her." He sat down, prepared for full disclosure. *"Tell me every little detail."*

"Can your young and innocent ears stand it?" Con propped his shoulder against the doorjamb. Deimos would be funny if he wasn't such a pain in the butt.

"I heard that." Deimos widened his yellow eyes in alarm. Probably just remembered Con's threat about what would happen if he listened in to thoughts that weren't his own. *"But I won't listen again. I'm permanently outta your mind. Promise."* His sly gaze said his promise meant squat. *"To answer your question, I can*

listen to it, but I can't watch it. Maybe when I get around to doing it myself I'll . . ." His voice faded away as he realized what he'd revealed.

Con bit back laughter. "You're a virgin? Let me get this straight. You're supposed to be this hotshot manipulator of humans' sex lives, and you've never done it yourself? Oh brother." He bit his lip to keep from grinning.

Deimos narrowed his eyes to tiny slits of fury. *"Laugh, jerk, and I turn you into a weed. We're wasting time here. Details. Now."*

"No." Con pushed away from the doorjamb just in case Deimos tried to follow through on his threat. "What Mandy and I do together is our own business."

"But what will I tell Sparkle?" He looked horrified.

Sparkle must be one scary lady if she could terrify the little guy like that. Con stomped down on his flicker of sympathy. He shrugged. "Tell her anything you want. Gotta go now." He closed the door on Deimos's whining, and then chuckled. A virgin. Who would've believed it.

All thoughts of Deimos fled, however, as he turned to find Mandy coming out of his bathroom. As he turned out the light and then rolled over to take her in his arms, he realized he hadn't felt this great in a long time. Ten years to be exact.

Mandy's singing had been known to scare small children, but that didn't stop her now. Life was good. She'd had an incredible night of love followed by a pro-

ductive day of shopping. When she got home from
Houston, she'd checked to make sure Con had followed
through on his promise to get rid of the blue butterflies.
Yep, gone.

They'd negotiated the blue butterfly deal after their
third round of wild sex. He'd agreed to paint out the butterflies, and she'd agreed to let the snakes stay. In her
new and giddier mood, she'd decided the snakes were
kind of cute.

Then she'd gone up to her room and changed into
the white shorts and purple clingy top she'd bought.
The new outfit symbolized a woman in transition. The
white was the old and elegant. The purple was the new
and bold.

Mandy ratcheted up the volume on her song at the
thought of her greatest triumph. After their fifth round
of, by then, more leisurely lovemaking, Con had agreed
to the cream walls. At first she thought he'd given in because he was too exhausted to argue, but he hadn't tried
to back out this morning.

Mandy was no dummy, though. She remembered
what happened when he agreed to paint the trim white.
She'd be on the lookout for a sneak attack.

Still singing . . . okay, it wasn't technically singing.
More like shouting off-key. But it made her feel good.
Still singing, she hung up the red dress she'd bought today. A sexy little piece of silk guaranteed to bring Con
to his knees. And who knew what erotic acts he could
perform while in a kneeling position. She was dying to
find out.

Her song wavered for a moment as she considered the path she was committing to. She was having too much fun. She was already too wrapped up in Con. What would happen when it was time to walk away from Con and Galveston? From the first moment she'd seen him again, she'd recognized the danger. But like the lemmings that came before her, she was swimming out to meet her fate. The strange thing? She didn't care. Mandy Harcourt had turned into a fatalist. What would happen, would happen.

The tiny voice of reason hiding somewhere in her empty brain made a last pitch for common sense. You can still back off. Sleep in your own room. Stick strictly to business. Nope, wasn't going to happen. She sang louder to drown out any other common sense her reason might throw at her.

Mandy was making so much noise she almost didn't hear the knock on her door. Con? She hurried to the door and flung it open.

Sparkle Stardust swayed into the room trailing a sexual aura bright enough to blind Mandy. Short black skirt. Low cut black top. Gold sandals. Sparkle didn't bend to seasonal fashion rules. She narrowed her spectacular amber gaze on Mandy.

"I was bringing a few plants up to Con's room when I heard the noise. It sounded like someone was murdering a cat slowly and painfully. I had to peek in to make sure Deimos hadn't made a nuisance of himself."

Mandy wanted to be angry about Sparkle's insult to her singing, but she knew it was true. "Plants? Why?"

She peered around Sparkle into the hall where a cart loaded with greenery stood. "A *few?* Sheesh, there must be thirty plants on that cart. Does Con know you're putting them in his room?"

"Twenty-five. And Con doesn't know. Do I look dumb? I'm going to put them in his room and run like hell." She strolled over to the bed and sat down. "But it's his own fault. I told Holgarth, who told the owner, about last night's spectacular sexual extravaganza. And the owner immediately demanded that all the castle's plants be transferred to Con's room so they could share in the overflow of sensual energy." She cast Mandy a curious glance. "That *is* where all the action is going down, isn't it?"

Mandy didn't bother closing her gaping mouth, because it would only fall open again. "Spectacular sexual extravaganza? Who told you this story?"

Sparkle shrugged. "An anonymous tip." Her eyes gleamed with barely suppressed excitement. "Tell me all about it."

"No. You tell me, then we'll both know." Who? Okay, she could eliminate Con. He didn't have loose lips. And no one else had been in the castle. Even with binoculars, no one could see much through the narrow arrow slits. Hidden cameras? Paranoid Central, Harcourt.

Sparkle waved Mandy's comment away. "This is no time for false modesty. I heard the foreplay lasted two hours."

"Two *hours*? I don't—"

"I heard you hung by your heels from the door frame

while Con brought you to a screaming climax with his tongue."

"*Door frame*? I never—"

"I heard he's twelve inches long, and once you slid your magic lips over him, it was all over. Woo woo, you go girl!"

"*Twelve* inches? He—"

"Well, as much as I'd like to hear more of the luscious details, especially the ones about your intense multiple orgasms that left you absolutely begging for mercy, I have to get those plants into Con's room before he shows up." She rose and hurried from the room.

Mandy knew her eyes must be glazed as she watched Sparkle unlock Con's door and take the plants inside. A few minutes later, she came out and locked the door behind her. Before leaving, she stuck her head into Mandy's room.

"The owner will be ecstatic. Sweetie Pie grew three inches. Let's hear it for great sex. Oh, and keep the purple. It's you."

Mandy heard Sparkle drag the cart into the elevator, but she didn't move from where she stood in the middle of the room. She was still standing there when Con walked in a few minutes later.

"Mmm. A purple top. I'm a corrupting influence, but corruption definitely looks great on you." He wrapped his arms around her and kissed the nape of her neck. "I met Sparkle as she was leaving. She looked seriously smug."

Mandy bent her neck to give him easier access. "And

well she should. Obviously, we had a lot more fun last night than we realized." She hit the high points and watched his eyes widen. "Oh, and we're doing such a great job with Sweetie Pie and Jessica, the owner wants us to work our magic on twenty-five more leafy friends."

Without speaking, Con strode from the room and unlocked his door. Mandy waited. Any second now . . .

"What the hell is this?" His outraged shout made her wince. He answered his own question. "It's a frickin' jungle."

Mandy joined him as he stared at the roomful of plants. "Why don't you jump into the shower, and then we can go get something to eat." She surreptitiously checked for hidden cameras.

Without comment, he headed for the bathroom, leaving her alone with the plants. "Sorry, girls, but you're out of luck tonight." No way could she make love here with Con tonight. Just the thought of all those leaves watching them gave her goose bumps. Good grief, Sparkle was making her crazy.

Con pulled out of Guido's parking lot onto Sea Wall Boulevard and drove toward the west end of the island. Over dinner, Mandy had tried to come up with the identity of the idiot spreading crazy rumors about their sex lives. Con pretended bafflement. Mandy wouldn't want to have the kids of a man who talked to cats.

Kids? His spontaneous thought startled him so much he almost drove his truck off the road. Where had *that* come from? From the little over a week they'd been together? Or had it lain dormant all these years, waiting to pop out and surprise him? And what did it really mean? You know what it means.

"Where're we going?" Mandy stared past him at the Gulf.

"To the place of perfect memories." He looked over at her and grinned. "The place of blue butterflies and black roses."

"Oh." And that's all she said until he eased the truck to the side of the road.

"Ten years have changed a few things." He stared at the line of beach houses. Ten years ago buildings were sparse this far west on the island.

"No kidding." He didn't miss the regret in her voice.

"With all the new houses, this beach is off-limits for the truck now, but we could get out and walk." It was off-limits for lovemaking, too, unless they wanted to outrage all the weekend visitors.

She shook her head, her gaze pensive. "I guess that old quote, 'You can never go home again,' is right."

"But you can make a new home." *With me.* Now that sounded like a man thinking about a serious commitment. It should scare him more than it did. "Guess we better get back to the castle."

"Right." Mandy stared straight ahead at the gathering darkness for the rest of the drive.

Con let quiet fill the cab, because he wasn't feeling too talkative either. Once inside the castle, he decided to work on his project for a while. The air around them was too emotionally charged. If he went upstairs with her, he'd want to make love to her, and that might lead to him admitting something that would make her uncomfortable.

"I'll be working down in the dungeon if you need me."

She simply nodded and headed for the elevator.

Exhaling deeply, he strode to the steps leading down to the dungeon, flipped on the lights, and descended to the Castle of Dark Dreams' ghoulish room of horror. Mandy would hate it. Dark gray walls. Dripping blood. Chains. Diabolic instruments of pain. He loved it.

Good thing she was still too busy with the rest of the castle to worry about this room. When she found time, she'd want him to paint the walls cream while she artistically arranged flowered rugs and potted plants to make it more homey.

All right, so he wasn't being fair. Except for her cream walls, she'd done a great job so far.

He'd barely started working when Deimos padded into the room. For once he was glad to see the cat. They had a major issue to deal with—whether Deimos lived or died. "Why the hell did you tell Sparkle those lies?"

Deimos blinked up at him. *"You told me to tell her anything I wanted. Hey, I did you a favor. I made you sound like the hottest thing to ever hit the island. Twelve inches, man. Women'll be lined up along Sea Wall Boulevard once the story spreads. So when are you guys doing it again?"*

"You're assuming you'll live to report on it?" He narrowed his gaze on Deimos, and the cat backed up.

"*You gotta tell me something.*" He padded over to take a closer look at Con's project. "*Or not. I have a great imagination.*"

Con took a threatening stride toward him.

Deimos looked a little nervous. "*Well, gotta go.*" He edged past Con to the door. "*Just so you know I'm really an okay guy, I'll tell you a secret. Mandy's thinking of staying.*" Then he was gone.

She was thinking of staying.

Mandy turned in front of her mirror to get a look at the red dress from all angles.

She'd done a mental tally sheet. Con on one side, New York on the other.

Hmm, the dress didn't cover very much. Good. It was all swirly and girly, and almost but not quite showed everything. A total tease.

Back to her tally sheet. Con—made her laugh. New York—her career. Con—made her mad, but she got a rush from arguing with him. New York—her career. Con—made her heart pound and her blood run hot. New York—her career. Con—made her feel beautiful, desired, and . . . Hmm . . . she saw a pattern forming here.

Ten years ago, she'd needed New York. She'd believed that true acceptance in the interior design field meant being successful in one of the greatest cities in the world. Did she still need New York? Did she still *want* New York if it meant leaving Con behind again? She'd pretty much answered that question on their drive back, but she'd needed her tally sheet to make it official.

She slipped on the red sandals she'd bought to go with the dress. Time to take a look at the dungeon. And even as she left her room, walked down the winding steps, hurried across the great hall, and descended the final set of steps to the dungeon, she wondered if Con wanted her to stay.

As soon as she stepped into the dungeon, she started talking. Nerves. The more she cared, the more power Con had to make her babble. "Ugh, I can't believe this room. Blood, gore, and really gruesome accessories. Can we say unoriginal? I—"

Silence wrapped around her as she saw what Con was working on. A large painting. She moved closer. Right in the middle was . . . ohmigod! Her bare butt. She knew it was hers because it had a blue butterfly on it. Mandy had already opened her mouth to shriek when she looked at Con for the first time. She closed her mouth.

Sure, he looked wary. How else would he look when faced with the Medusa? But there was something else in his eyes. A vulnerability she hadn't seen before. She took a second look at the mural.

If she could get past her butt, she'd admit he had talent. The scene showed a sunny day, and in the background was a hill with a castle that looked a lot like the Castle of Dark Dreams. In the forefront was a meadow surrounded by trees and filled with bluebonnets. One huge oak dominated the scene. Two lovers lay among the flowers, half hidden behind the tree. Too bad the wrong half was showing. Her bare behind was front and center. For the first time, she took a closer look at the man. There wasn't as much of him showing, because her bottom hogged the show. But when she looked really close, she saw the black rose on his bare hip.

"And you were inspired to create this why?" She would *not* shout.

"I started this the first day you arrived. I figured it'd look great on one of the great hall's walls." A smile tugged at the corners of his mouth.

Over my dry and shriveled corpse. "Uh-huh. I guess that's why you agreed to the cream walls without a fight." Maybe she was finally getting a sense of humor about her behind, because the whole thing was kind of funny.

"Well, I figured you deserved to have three walls painted the way you wanted them, because this baby would be hanging on the fourth." He put down the brush he still held in his hand and moved toward her. "I decided to paint myself into the picture three days ago."

"This painting yourself into the picture, does it have a symbolic meaning?" She forced herself to breathe normally.

"Yes." He held her gaze. "I don't want you out there by yourself. I want to be with you."

Mandy exhaled the breath she'd sworn she wouldn't hold. She glanced around the room again. "This room, as gothic as it is, does have possibilities." She twirled in front of him, and knew exactly what he could see as the skirt flared. Panties were so nonessential in her seduction plans. "I wore my best dress, and I came to play."

His eyes darkened. "It's the sexiest dress I've ever seen. Take it off."

"Nope." She hoped her smile was suitably provocative. "You owe me for this painting. I've always fantasized about having a hunky man chained naked and helpless in my very own dungeon."

"And you were naked, too?"

He looked so hopeful. Too bad she'd have to disappoint him. "Never. In my fantasy, I keep my clothes on. It's a power thing."

"And then what happens?" He looked disappointed but intrigued.

"I torture you with my mouth and, umm, other body parts until you scream for mercy." Her smile widened. "And then, sometimes, if you've amused me, I free you."

His gaze darkened. "I wouldn't count on me screaming for mercy any time soon."

Mandy brightened. "No? Great. I hope it takes a long time." She moved up close and tugged at his T-shirt. "Take it off."

Without comment, he pulled it over his head. The pure visual impact of his wide muscular chest always wrung a small startled gasp from her. You'd think she'd be used to it by now. Maybe some natural wonders never lose their ability to awe.

Still silent, he discarded his sandals, and slid his jeans over his lean hips. Red briefs. Why was she not surprised? And she absolutely had not bought a red dress as a cheap ploy to turn him on. It hadn't been cheap at all, and American Express would back her up.

He hooked his thumbs over the briefs, but before he could slide them down, she put her hands over his thumbs. "I'd like to do the honors."

Con nodded and dropped his hands to his side. Kneeling on the concrete floor, Mandy pulled them over his powerful thighs and then let them fall to the floor where he kicked them out of the way.

Mmm. While the thinking part of Conleth Maguire was probably still analyzing data on her fantasy's possibilities, his primitive center for sexual gratification had already decided that, hey, kinky is fun, and was rising to the challenge.

"You know, I'm glad those rumors that you're twelve inches of long, strong man are off by a couple of inches." She stroked his erection with the tips of her fingers. So much power to please sheathed in smooth taut skin. "Because according to those same rumors, I can fit every studly inch of you in my mouth. That would officially make me the babe with the biggest mouth in Texas."

She watched him bite back his laughter. "If you keep mentioning my studliness and your mouth in the same sentence, you might have a very short fantasy."

"Right. All serious here." She narrowed her eyes and

thinned her lips until she morphed into Super Vixen. "Up against the wall, animal." She glanced at the wall. "What're those manacles made of?"

"Plastic. Chains are plastic, too." He backed against the wall and waited expectantly. "I won't be able to put them on myself."

"I guess I'll have to get close to you and do it myself." She offered him an evil leer.

Swaggering to where he stood, she pressed herself against his bare body as she reached for the manacles. "Spread your arms and legs." Standing on her toes, she clipped the plastic cuffs on his wrists. When she was finished, she rubbed her breasts against his chest, lightly pinched each of his nipples, and then bent over to shackle his ankles. She maintained her bent position long enough for Con to realize that bras didn't figure into her seduction plans either.

Finally straightening, she brushed her lips across his. "Where to start, where to start?" Mandy smiled her most wicked smile. "You have so many things to pay for." She trailed kisses across his chest, pausing to flick each nipple with her tongue. All of this nipple action was making her feel . . . anxious. It was also setting off some minor tremors in parts of her body susceptible to major quakes.

"Okay, had enough. Let me go." A thin sheen of sweat was forming on his body.

She made a small moue of disappointment. "I can't let you go yet. I haven't even started to exact payment." Mandy slid her tongue down the middle of his chest and over his flat stomach. "That's for the snakes with blue butterflies on their tails." The minor tremors were escalating to anticipatory clenching, and her nipples were experiencing extraordinary sensitivity. All signs of a coming eruption. She frowned. Wait, eruption meant volcano and trembling meant earthquake. Oh, what the hell. The earth would move. That's all she needed to know.

"Push me too far, Harcourt, and you . . . probably won't regret it." He looked desperate, but loving it.

Dropping to her knees again, Mandy glided her fingers along his inner thighs, and then bent forward to gently kiss the flesh around his arousal. "This is for painting my bare behind in your picture. The only reason I'm showing some mercy is because you painted yourself beside me." And because her own body was making some pretty specific demands. She needed to speed things up.

"You're killing me with your mercy, wicked woman." His breathing was taking on a raspy sound.

"Thank you. We do what we can." She cupped his balls in her palms and circled each with the tip of her tongue.

"And this is for making me want you again." Circling his erection with her tongue, she worked her way up to the head. Then she slid her lips over the head and swirled her tongue in ever tightening circles—teasing, tormenting."

He groaned and then sucked in his breath. For a moment the room was completely silent. As he exhaled sharply, she slid her mouth down his length, taking him deeply. Slowly, she began the rhythmic in and out motion that would drive him beyond control.

Talk about control . . . The male taste of him, the heated scent of him, and the sensation of her mouth sliding over his flesh, made her want to stand up, wrap her legs around his hips, and take him right there against the wall. Whoa, she was losing it.

"Stop now, Mandy. I'm not going to last much longer." He sounded seriously upset by that fact. "Set me free."

She leaned back on her heels and gazed up into his eyes. Heat, hunger, and an emotion she wasn't quite sure of moved in them. Well, here went all or nothing.

"This is the last thing you have to pay for, my Druid." She laid her palm over the black rose on his hip. "Your special magic made me love you, Con." She replaced her palm with her mouth. And carefully traced the flower with her tongue.

"Set. Me. Free. Forget it. I'll do it myself." With a growl that would've thrown fear even into the heart of Holgarth, he broke the plastic manacles.

Uh-oh. She scrambled to her feet. "Gee, they don't make dungeon equipment like they used to."

That's all she had time to say before he was on her. He spun her around, and before she could yelp her alarm, he'd unzipped her dress and it was floating to the floor. Since everything else was gone, she kicked off her sandals.

"I'll never make it up those steps. So we have a choice, sweet-heat. We can make love on the concrete or do it standing up. I'm a softy at heart, so you get to choose." His breath was hot against her neck.

The concrete biting into her behind? Not likely. "The wall sounds sensational. But do it fast before I self-destruct."

She braced herself against the wall while he gripped her bottom and lifted her off her feet. Wrapping her legs around his hips, she put her head back and whooped her joy as he drove into her. *Faster, harder, faster, harder.* The words ran together in her mind as the pressure built, built, and then exploded. The earth rocked and rolled, the volcano spewed fire into the sky, and she screamed her completion to the universe.

Her legs slid to the floor, but they sort of wobbled. Con kept his arms locked around her, and she could feel the thump of his heart as an extension of her own heart.

His breath was still coming in painful gasps. "I love you, Mandy Harcourt. Marry me, and you can paint all the walls of our house cream for the rest of our lives."

He loved her that much? Mandy leaned away from him so she could see his eyes. She knew he'd probably see the shine of tears in hers, but it didn't matter. She was just so damn happy. "Really?"

"Really." He scooped up their clothes scattered around the dungeon. "Let's get upstairs so we can generate some plant growth."

"We can hang your painting on one of the walls of

our house." She raised her arms as he slid her dress over
her head and zipped it up.

"Great." He picked up each of her feet to slip on her
sandals.

"I'll wear a red wedding dress." That would make the
sluts in her basement cheer.

"You can wear cream if you want." He must be feeling mellow.

"We have to invite Holgarth and Sparkle to the wedding." Mandy frowned. "I know it's unusual, but I want
Sparkle to bring Deimos. I mean, he sort of helped to
bring us together."

Con mumbled something as he pulled his T-shirt over
his head. She'd take it as a yes.

"Do you think the owner would let us take Sweetie
Pie and Jessica home with us?" She was feeling gener-
ous toward the world.

"No. Absolutely not."

Well, that was definite. "Sheesh, you didn't have to
shout."

"Look at me, Mandy." He tipped her chin up so she
had to meet his gaze. "Besides loving me for the rest of
your life, there's one other thing I'd like you to do."

"Anything." Well, almost anything. She still wouldn't
paint the castle walls red.

"I want you to model for me. I want to paint pictures
of you in every mood, with sun shining on your face,
and shadows turning you all sensual and mysterious."
He stroked the side of her face with the back of his hand.

She widened her eyes and slid her tongue across her

lower lip. "I don't care where or how you paint me, but just make sure of one thing."

"What?"

"Always color me wicked."

THE
FIXER-UPPER

MaryJanice Davidson

For Stacy,
who gave me the idea

ACKNOWLEDGMENTS

Thanks as always to my family for their support. And especially to my sister, who never minds when I cancel our plans so I can finish a story.

AUTHOR'S NOTE

There are no such things as ghosts, which only means that I have never seen one.

He dodged, laughing, and lost his footing. The fun stopped as the stairs rushed up at him. Adrenaline was dumped into his system but there was nothing to clutch onto, nothing to slow his fall. The last thing he heard, besides his neck breaking between the third and fourth vertebra, was his sister, screaming.

He did plenty of screaming himself, but no one could hear him, and no one could see him.

He stayed gone for a long time.

CHAPTER ◆ ONE

"And if you would sign here . . . and initial here . . . and sign here . . . and here again . . ."

Cathy signed and initialed until her hand cramped. Catherine Sarah Wyth. CSW. Thank goodness for all those little red Sign Here notes, or she would have been lost. Even *with* her Realtor.

"And here's a check."

"What a pleasant surprise," she said, and she meant it. The house she was buying was already draining money; it was nice that they'd overestimated closing costs. She could buy a new couch! Well, half a couch. A cushion, maybe. "Is that it? Are we done?"

Her Realtor, John Barnes, looked across the table at the owner's lawyer, John Barney. Like *that* never got confusing. "I think we're okay, here, how about you, John?"

"Fine, John. Cathy"—John #1 stood to shake her hand—"I hope you'll be very happy in your new house. I have to say it's nice that something positive could come out of tragedy."

"Thanks, John," she replied, barely listening—she was too busy mentally redecorating her new fixer-upper. Then she shook hands with John #2. "John." She scooped up the folder with roughly 1,212 pieces of paperwork, and carefully tucked her check in her purse. "Okay, well, I guess I'll go check out the house."

My new house.

"Congratulations," John #2 said.

"Good luck," John #1 said.

"Thank you, gentlemen. Have a good one." She skipped out the doorway, remembered herself, then said to hell with it and skipped the rest of the way to her car. The last time she had skipped to anything she had had a consuming interest in Super Balls and Lik 'Em Aid. She still liked Lik 'Em Aid, but everything else had changed.

She drove straight to 1001 Tyler Avenue in St. Paul, Minnesota, parked in *her* driveway, and stared up at *her* house.

Her house.

Even now, she couldn't believe it was real. All those years of saving, of making a pair of shoes last two years and a suit last four, of going without nice vacations and pricey clothes and fancy cars, lobster tails and caviar—not that she could abide fish eggs, but still—had finally paid off. She was a home owner.

She climbed out of her car—yet another sacrifice to

her new home; it was a 1994 Ford Taurus and it wheezed in the cold—and stood in her yard, then strolled around the—her—property.

The turrets, in particular, delighted her. Like something Rapunzel would hang out in. And the mini-porch up on the roof. The bay windows, the huge kitchen—it seemed especially huge after years of apartment efficiencies.

It definitely needed work. For one thing, the house wasn't really pink . . . over the years, the deep red had faded. It had probably looked a lot nicer in 1897. The porch steps looked downright dangerous—a lawsuit waiting to happen—and the fence looked like broken teeth. The garden had been, to put it politely, overrun.

It wasn't surprising—the woman who had sold the house to Cathy had been, at rough guess, a thousand years old. Not that she had seen the woman, but Cathy knew she was an original descendent of the family who had built the home. Spry she was not. The house had, understandably, eventually been too much for her.

That was all right. That was, in fact, the only reason Cathy had been able to afford a 2,800 square-foot home at her age, on her salary. And she had wanted this place the moment she saw it on the Edina Realty website. Not because it was big, although that was nice. But because it was a home. It had character. And if it needed work, well, Cathy had never been afraid to get her hands dirty.

She heard a pounding and looked over to the yard on her left. A shirtless fellow had his back to her, had something set up on those whatchamacall'ems—the things you set something on when you were going to hammer them. Or something. Horses? No, that couldn't be right.

Anyway, the guy was really pounding away, and sweat was gleaming across his broad back. It was only May, but Cathy felt herself start to sweat in response. Oofta. Broad back, narrow waist, tool belt, faded jeans. It was like watching a Bowflex commercial.

He turned, still holding the hammer, and their gaze met across the low hedge. How romantic. She could see how dark his eyes were from all the way across her yard. Gorgeous brown eyes, full mouth, aquiline nose. Strong chin, long neck, broad yummy shoulders. His chest was lightly furred, the hair tapering down to a line leading straight to his, um, belt. He looked like a moody prince, out to do a little carpentry work before running the country.

New house. No more renting. A decent temp job. A yummy next-door neighbor. Oh, lucky, lucky day!

"Well, fuckin' A," her prince said. "A new neighbor. Fuckin' great! Hey, how the fuck are ya?"

Oh dear, she thought.

CHAPTER ◆ TWO

"So you're a temp worker, huh? Like a new job every week?"

"Something like that." She topped off her neighbor's water glass. Well, water Dixie cup.

"Can't hold a job, huh?" He guffawed, throwing his long neck back. She smiled thinly and said nothing. The truth was, she hated to be tied down. Trying a new job every month or so suited her perfectly. "Well, that's a bitch."

"Not really. I'm sorry, I didn't get your name . . . ?"

"Ken Allen."

"I'm Cathy."

"Aww, Ken and Cathy, that's kinda cute."

"Not really. Well, I've got a lot of work to do . . ."

"I'll help you move in," he said immediately. She noticed it wasn't a question.

"That's okay. You're busy, and my friends are coming over tomorrow to—"

"You gotta have some stuff with you. Chicks always bring shit with them."

"As a matter of fact, I do have some shit with me, but you don't have to—"

He ignored her, got up, and moved toward the kitchen door. "I'll go get it."

She trailed after him, uncomfortable and silent. The truth was, she never knew how to behave around strong-willed—okay, obnoxious—people. She herself was more the quiet type. Her best friend was strong-willed enough for the both of them. Give her a book and a cup of tea and she was in heaven. She tended to stay out of the way of such people. Then she'd spend days despising herself for her cowardice, but she was definitely a low-road kind of girl, and that was all there was to it.

"What a piece of shit," he said upon seeing her car.

"Thank you," she replied neutrally.

"Friend of mine owns a Chevy dealership. I'll get you set up."

"Thanks, but that's really not—"

"I'll call him for you tomorrow."

"Thanks, but frankly, after buying a new house, the last thing I need to do is—"

"Go pop the trunk."

Grinding her teeth, she did so. He's just being nice, she told herself. A good neighbor.

"Gotta tell you," he said, lugging her boxes and suitcases inside with zero strain—ooh, those rippling muscles— "it's nice to have that fucking old bitch out of here."

"That's so sweet." She'd never met someone so equally handsome and obnoxious. The foul words that kept coming out of that sinfully sullen mouth nearly made her gasp. "And by sweet, I mean vaguely disturbing."

"What?"

"Nothing."

"Nice to have somebody you can look at, you know? You know, you'd be almost cute if you cut your hair and didn't button your shirt all the way up."

"Okay. Well, thanks," she said as he set down the last of the boxes in her living room. "I'm sure you want to get back to your project."

"Fuckin' A. I'll see you around, Cathy."

Why did that sound like a threat? She shrugged it off as single-woman paranoia and set about emptying the few boxes she had brought for Closing Day.

CHAPTER ◆ THREE

"Oh my God!" her best friend and worst enemy, Nikki, gasped and nearly swooned. "Who is *that?*"

"My next door neighbor. You'd like him; he's vulgar."

"Don't tease." Nikki lasciviously wiggled her eyebrows. "Day-amn! Cute, cute, *cute!*"

"Knock yourself out." Then, louder as Ken approached, she said, "Good morning."

"Hey." He nodded to Nikki. "Hey."

"Nikki, this is my next door neighbor, Ken Allen. Ken, this is my best friend, Nikki Sheridan."

"Hey," he repeated.

"Well, hi there. Nice to meet you."

"Do you *own* a shirt?" Cathy asked politely. Shirtless Ken was once again flawlessly, if casually, attired in work boots, jeans, and a tool belt.

"It's too fuckin' hot," he complained. "You're lucky I'm even helping you move all your shit."

"So, so lucky," she replied, annoyed at the amused look on Nikki's face. They had known each other since the fourth grade and were more like sisters than friends—like a close family member, she often wanted to strangle Nikki, or at least banish her. The flip side was, if anyone ever threatened Nikki, Cathy would take a baseball bat to their frontal lobe. "Thank you for coming over."

"Yeah." He turned his back to them and trotted down the porch steps, sidestepping her other friends and wrestling the television out of the back of the rental van.

"I said it before and I'll say it again: day-amn!"

"He's obnoxious," Cathy muttered under her breath.

"Like you could do so much better. If you could, sunshine, you would have by now."

"Here comes the 'you're not getting any younger' speech."

"Well, you're not. You're on the wrong side of your twenties, girlfriend, and you've got a golden opportunity right next door."

"He's not what I would call golden," she commented.

"Golden tan," Nikki said dreamily. "God, he must work out ten hours a day. In the sun. Getting sweaty. All sweaty in the blazing sun. Ummm . . ."

"Go for it. You two were made for each other."

"Meaning I'm an obnoxious bitch," she said cheerfully, taking no offense. "Thanks tons. Hey, he wouldn't be coming over here if he didn't think you were cute."

"I'm not cute," she said coldly. "Kittens are cute. I'm a grown woman."

"Says the five foot nothing shrimp-o," Nikki said, smugly secure with her five feet, ten inches. "You've got to get over the cute thing. It's not a dirty word, y'know. You're short, you're gorgeous, women pay hundreds of dollars to make their hair as curly—"

"Frizzy."

"—as yours is naturally, and you've got Sinatra blue eyes. You're like a gypsy princess with Sinatra eyes."

"Why, Nikki. That was almost poetic." Nikki always saw her friends as gorgeous beauties, which sounded like a good quality, but really was a little on the annoying side. Particularly if you were the type who knew you weren't beautiful. "I didn't know you cared."

Nikki ignored the jibe. "Now you're getting pissy because he's attracted to you?"

"He doesn't know me."

"Hardly anybody does, sugarplum. You're kind of famous for keeping us all at arm's length."

"It certainly doesn't work on you."

"No chance, baby," she said, grinning. "I know I'm your hero."

"I suspect Ken's interest in me is strictly of the novelty type."

"It's what what of the what?"

"I'm here," she explained, "like Everest. So he's interested."

"So? That's as good a reason as any to get sweaty with a sexy neighbor."

"Nikki . . ."

"Come on, let's get you moved in."

Nikki was right, Cathy thought, following her friend to the van. She is my hero. I could never be so relaxed, so fun. So obnoxious and blunt. But I'm not going for Ken, no matter how much she nags me. It just wasn't meant to be.

However, I have no plans to buy him a shirt in the near future.

CHAPTER ◆ FOUR

She couldn't find her keys, which was infuriating and, worse, made her want to cry with frustration. She hated, *hated* not being able to find things. It's why she was still unpacking at 3:00 A.M. It's why she decided it was a good time to drive to the local 24-hour supermarket and stock the fridge, so when she got up in the morning—later today, rather—she could have her toast and yogurt and tea.

"Goddammit!" she cried, running her fingers through her frizz—yes, that's right, *frizz*, never mind how often Nikki admired her hair and said it was curly and, ugh, cute. "Where are you?"

She had a place for them, of course—the drawer in the writing desk in her foyer. That was where they belonged. That was where they *should* be. But she'd lent them to Karl so he could move her car out of the way of the van, and who knew where he'd put them? Karl was an engineer, so you'd think he was reliable, but the fact was, he was infamous for losing his checkbook, his keys, his contact lens case. What had she been thinking, letting him take her keys?

She'd looked everywhere. Everywhere. If she didn't find them soon, she was calling Karl, and never mind how late it was. He was probably up, anyway, playing another marathon session of War Craft.

She started going through the kitchen drawers again, which was stupid because she *knew* they weren't there. Then, oddly, she heard a familiar jingle. She turned . . . and froze in place as her keys bumped down the back stairs and slid across the floor, stopping two inches from her left big toe.

She was tired.

She was tired, and it had been a long day—a day not over yet—and she was very, very tired. And, apparently, the proud new owner of a haunted house.

"No I'm not," she said aloud. "I'm just tired. They were probably there all the time and I—I made a little mind movie to explain how they got there."

The keys, resting beside her foot, suddenly raised themselves up two inches and shook, jangling merrily.

She ran out the back door, but not before she bent and scooped them up.

* * *

"Ken! Ken, let me in!" She hammered on the door until her fist went numb. "Ken, I've got to come in!"

He opened the door and blinked at her, swaying slightly. She could smell the beer before he even opened his mouth. "Say, Cathy, hey-hey. Whatchoo doing here?"

She bulled past him and stood in his kitchen, wrapping her arms around herself for comfort. "I—something weird happened and—I'm sorry to bother you so late. It's just I don't know anybody in the neighborhood except you and I—I didn't know what to do."

"Thass okay." He was shirtless, and pantsless, splendidly arrayed in navy blue boxers. No tool belt this time. His hairy legs, she wasn't too rattled to note, were long, lean, and smoothly muscled. "M'glad you came over." He lurched toward her and clumsily pawed for her breasts, but due to his extreme inebriation, and her extreme shortness, he groped her shoulders instead. "Less go upstairs? Hmmm?"

"On second thought," she said, removing his hand, "I will take my chances with the ghost. Good night." She managed to evade his drunken gropings and soon found herself back in her house. Her haunted house.

"Okay," she said out loud. "Let's think about this." Going to Ken had been a stupid mistake—a stupid, hysterical, childish mistake. For God's sake. She was a grown woman and what had she done? Run away like a coward and shook like a puppy in a stranger's kitchen, a stranger she was beginning to really dislike.

Because her keys had moved by themselves. Stupid, stupid!

"It wasn't necessarily a bad thing," she continued aloud. "The keys showed up, right?"

A definitive rap, as if unseen knuckles had knocked on the ceiling.

"Okay," she said again, taking a deep, steadying breath. "Are you one of my friends playing a joke? I promise I won't get mad."

Two raps.

"This was your house?"

One rap.

"Well, it's . . . it's my house now," she said with a firmness she most definitely did not feel. "I mean to say, I will be living here from now on. I-I hope that's all right."

One rap.

"Good. My name is Cathy. If one rap equals A, and two raps equal B, and three equals C, and so forth, what is your name?"

J-A-C-K.

"Well, it's . . . it's nice to meet you," she said, feeling foolish. Part of her could hardly believe this was happening. It *had* to be a joke. Because otherwise, her beloved pink Victorian was haunted, and did she really want to share living space with the dead?

No. She did not.

"I'm . . . I'm going out now. To get groceries. Will you be here when I get back?"

Nothing.

"Hello?"

Nothing.

Feeling both disappointed and relieved, Cathy managed to walk, not run, out of the house this time.

CHAPTER ◆ FIVE

No one named Jack had ever lived in her house.

Cathy had spent her lunch break doing extensive research and web surfing into land, deeds, home ownership, and spirits. She quickly determined her ghost was not a poltergeist, and did not seem malevolent, but she had less luck finding out who it—he—was. But apparently, his silence after the evening's excitement was not atypical: manifesting seemed to really tire out a ghost.

The question was: did she mind?

She did not know; it was too early to tell. All it—he—had done was talk to her and produce her keys. Then nothing for the rest of the night, or the entire next day—Sunday—or this morning.

She couldn't discuss this with Nikki, because her friend had a strong streak of practicality. If she couldn't see it or touch it, it wasn't real. Cathy, however, tended to believe her senses. Her keys moved by themselves. Someone had spelled out the letters J, A, C, and K. If it wasn't a practical joke, which she had not entirely ruled out—though if it *was* a joke, no one had come forward and it was going on too long—then she was prepared to believe her house was haunted. It was certainly old enough to house a spirit or two.

She thought about calling her real-estate agent, John #1, then immediately decided against it. She'd been living in her new house less than seventy-two hours. It was a little early to go running for help.

And whatever would she tell him? "Hello, John, the house you sold me is haunted and I . . . I : . ." What? Wanted a refund? Not hardly. She wasn't going back to pouring money down the rent rathole. Not ever. She had felt like a drone bee in a hive, living in those low-personality apartment complexes.

She decided to go about her business as usual, and see what the ghost—if it *was* a ghost—did next.

"Perfect," she said as lightning crashed outside her window. It was a dark and stormy night. No, really. "That's just perfect."

She had finished the unpacking and was almost swaying with exhaustion. But it was finished, all finished. A place for everything and she had put everything in its place. Now the house felt a little more like her house.

A little. She still couldn't believe it when she pulled into the driveway and realized this was her house. She owned it and lived there and it was hers. She supposed the feeling of euphoric surprise would go away someday. It was almost a shame.

The storm had started about three hours ago, and was building up to a rare fury—rare for St. Paul, anyway. As long as it wasn't a blizzard, most Minnesotans didn't get too annoyed by the weather. That might change, today, especially if—

The lights went out.

"And again," she said aloud. "Perfect." Rats and double rats. Where had she unpacked candles? After a moment's thought, she remembered they were in one of the kitchen drawers, as were the—

"One more time," she said as she heard a kitchen drawer open by itself, heard things clink and shift around, heard a candle rolling in the dark toward her. "Perfect."

She looked down and, when lightning flashed again, saw two candles bump up against her foot, along with a small box of matches she'd grabbed the last time she'd had sushi at Kikugawa.

"Thank you," she said. Testing, she added, "Thank you, Jack."

No response.

She bent, picked up a candle, lit it, used the lit candle to light the other one, stood. She still had a very real sense of unreality about the whole business, but one thing was certain: having a ghost around could be handy.

CHAPTER ◆ SIX

Her weekly duty was almost completed. Ah, to be so close to the end, and yet have it remain so tantalizingly out of reach.

"Cathy? You still there?"

"Still here, Dad," she confirmed. Her father lived in Missouri with her Wicked Stepmother, or W for short.

Not that there was a thing wrong with Kitty Wyth (if one overlooked the absurdity of referring to a fifty-eight-year-old woman as "Kitty", which was difficult even during the best of times).

Cathy had lost her mother to breast cancer when she herself was barely into puberty—possibly the worst time to lose a parent. And she was not prepared to welcome anyone who was there to take her mother's place. Thus, Kitty had been dubbed W and that was it, that was all there was to it. She was Wicked, sleeping in Cathy's mother's bed. She was The Stepmother—not the true Mrs. Wyth—and that was the end of it.

"Maybe Kitty and I should come down to see you. Maybe Labor Day Weekend," her father suggested doubtfully. Warm family get-togethers were not their thing. This was, Cathy knew, entirely her fault. W had done nothing wrong; had tried, many many times, to make Cathy feel included and loved.

If she could not have her mother's love, Cathy did not want the love of a grown woman named Kitty.

This, she knew, made her a bad person.

"Well," she replied, not actually answering her father, "it was nice talking to you."

"Yeah. You, too." He hung up. Her father never said good-bye.

She walked into the kitchen to hang up the phone and saw one of her mother's china plates on the table, with one of the frosted sugar cookies she'd picked up at the bakery that morning. Beside the plate was a small glass of milk.

"Right, Jack. Because I need that on my thighs," she joked.

"Who are you talking to?"

Cathy turned and saw Nikki standing in front of her screen door. "Myself," she replied easily. She ignored Jack's indignant knock and let Nikki in. "Oh, good, you've started dropping in without calling first. I was afraid you wouldn't pick up any bad habits this year."

"Go fuck yourself," her friend replied cheerfully. "I was in the neighborhood—that bakery is kick ass—and thought I'd come over." She held up a white wax paper bag and shook it.

"Oh no," Cathy said.

"Oh yes! Cream puffs!"

"You're evil," she replied, but took the bag.

"And you're too thin. Like, it's time to be drinking Ensure too thin." Nikki smacked herself on the flank. "Someday, when you grow up, you might possibly top out at over a hundred pounds, and then people will start to take you seriously."

Cathy laughed. Yes, *that* was the problem, oh yes indeed, no one took her seriously. Ha!

"Soooooo," Nikki said, sitting down and drinking Cathy's milk, "have you jumped Shirtless Ken yet?"

"I'm pretty sure that's not his real name," she teased.

"Avoid the question a little more! So, I'm guessing no."

"You would be guessing correctly. In addition to his many other odious qualities, which are legion, he drinks."

"Oh."

"A lot."

"Well, drinks like, hey, come in and have a beer? You know, like normal people? Or drinks like, hey, come in and help me finish this keg?"

"I have no idea because, thankfully, I don't know him well enough to make that judgment. He mentioned losing his license the other day. DUIs."

"Ouch. Still, that doesn't mean he'd, you know, suck in the sack."

Cathy rolled her eyes. Neither rain nor sleet nor substance abuse would prevent Nikki from pushing inappropriate partners on a friend. "Thankfully, I have no idea if that's true."

"Well, get on it, Cath. You've gotta strike while the bird is in the bush."

"And you've got to stop mixing your metaphors. I cannot *believe* you're pushing me toward this man, whom you know perfectly well is totally inappropriate for me. For any right-thinking woman."

"First off, real people don't say 'whom.' Stop saying 'whom.' Second, what? Like you've got so many great other options?"

"There is more to life," she said sternly, "than sex."

"There *is?*" Nikki looked shocked, which made Cathy laugh again. "Get out!"

"I'd like to, but this is my kitchen."

"Yeah, brag a little more, creep. I still can't believe you actually own property."

"I can't, either," she confessed.

"I suppose you're already plotting to redo the fence? Dig up the garden? Fix the gate?"

"Yes, yes, and yes."

"And the fact that you don't know a drill bit from a dildo isn't going to stop you?"

"Well, no," she said, and burst out laughing.

"Just checking." Nikki downed a cream puff while prowling around the main floor, eventually pronouncing it, "Absurdly neat. Finished unpacking already, huh? Yech."

"We can't all take eighteen months." Cathy shuddered. She'd helped Nikki move last winter and the woman *still* had boxes stacked all over the guest bedroom. "Seriously, Nikki, how about if I come over and—"

"No no no no no no *no*."

"No?"

"You're *not* coming over and unpacking for me. No way! I can never find a damned thing after you've cleaned. You have to hide everything."

"I did not hide the vacuum cleaner," she replied sharply. "It was in your hall closet—an eminently suitable location, I might add, and—"

"Blah-blah-blah. So, what are we doing today?"

Cathy sighed. Nikki was annoying, blunt, rude, infuriating, and her oldest friend. She would do well to keep in mind that Nikki put up with *her* personality quirks as well. And almost always without complaining. Well, sometimes without complaining. Well . . .

"I didn't know we were doing anything today," she replied. "What did you have in mind?"

"Going over to see how badly Shirtless Ken is hung over," Nikki said promptly. "Then invite him out to lunch. Let's take him to one of those No Shirt, No Shoes, No Service places, just for fun."

Cathy laughed again, unwillingly. The most annoying thing about Nikki—and this was really saying something—was her completely absurd way of looking at life. Because she had not been joking. "How about we don't do that, instead?"

"Oh, fine, you pick, then." Nikki took off her baseball cap—the one with the puzzling yet eternally fascinating logo GOT MAMMARIES?—fiddled with her long, straight blond hair for a moment, then tucked it all up under the cap. It never ceased to amaze Cathy how much hair Nikki managed to hide. Normally it hung down to the statuesque beauty's waist.

Maybe that's why Nikki saw all her friends as beautiful, Cathy mused. Because she herself looked like an escapee from a *Sports Illustrated* swimsuit issue. Ridiculous, but there it was.

"As long as it's something fun," Nikki was ordering. "Which means *no* libraries, *no* bookstores, and *no* bed-and-breakfast tours."

"No tractor pulls, either."

"Like I'd go to one in this heat," Nikki retorted, which was, Cathy felt, entirely beside the point.

CHAPTER ◆ SEVEN

"Ooooh," Nikki said when they pulled into Cathy's driveway four hours later. "Company."

"God *dammit*," Cathy said, and pulled the emergency brake with a yank. Nikki's car, a standard transmission, promptly stalled. Annoying habit of Nikki's Number 672: the woman insisted on being driven everywhere. "I told him. I *told* him."

"Uh-oh. I'm sensing a personal space violation."

"How the *hell* did he get in?"

"Whoa with the potty mouth! A 'dammit' and a 'hell' on the same day? Cripes. Poor slob doesn't know who he's messing with."

"You're right about that," Cathy snarled.

"Now Cath. I'm sure"—Nikki said, scrambling out of the car and hurrying after her—"he's just trying to help. You should be, um, flattered."

"Flattered?"

"Okay, intensely annoyed. Aw, come on, give him a break . . . he's so cute!"

"People have been making allowances based on his appearance his entire life, I've no doubt." Cathy pushed the front door open and practically leapt into the foyer. "I have had enough."

Her worst fears were realized: Shirtless Ken had lugged a stepladder, tool box, and various implements that required plug-ins into her living room. He was currently up on the ladder, poking a screwdriver at her 123-year-old chandelier.

Which he had offered to fix the day she moved in.

Which she had politely refused.

And now he had snuck, had waited until she was gone and *snuck into her home,* on the pretense of "helping" her, and that was . . . that was just really . . . that was . . .

"Ken!" she bawled, and later decided that's why she felt such guilt and why she made the series of disastrous decisions. Because if she hadn't yelled, the rest of it might never have happened.

Startled—which was stupid, hadn't he heard them drive up?—Ken flinched. The screwdriver went in a little too far. Shirtless Ken was suddenly galvanized as electric current slammed through him.

Cathy had just enough time to start toward him and think, *don't touch him, knock him off the ladder with something wooden—a broom?,* when he toppled off the ladder and hit the living room carpet so hard a cloud of dust rose in the air.

"Holy shit!" Nikki had time to gasp, before Cathy seized her arm in a claw-like grip. "Ow!"

Then Cathy hissed, "9-1-1!"

While Nikki grabbed for her cell phone, Cathy crossed the room, seized Ken by his shirtless shoulder, and hauled him over on his back. His eyes were open, staring at nothing. His chest didn't rise and fall. There was blood on his face, blood had foamed from his nose, but it wasn't moving, wasn't leaking. It was just there.

Cathy did not pray—she believed in God, but felt He had a strict "every man, woman, and child for themselves" policy—but she had time to think, Please God, not another ghost in this place. Then she started mouth-to-mouth and CPR.

"Well, he was clinically dead for a good minute," the doctor told her an hour later. "Lucky for him you were there, Miss Wyth."

"I don't think he's gonna see it exactly that way," Nikki cracked. Cathy shot her a look and the taller woman immediately stuffed the rest of the Hershey's bar in her mouth. "Gmmf nnnf unnf."

Cathy took a deep breath and faced the resident. "How long will he be here, doctor?"

"Well, we'll keep him overnight for observation," she said. She was a short woman who was probably twenty-five but looked forty-five. Sleep-deprived didn't begin to cover it. She blinked at Cathy through glasses that made her look like a tired owl. "But you can take him home in the morning."

"*I* can?"

"Yes, he's listed you on all his forms."

"But I'm just his neighbor!"

"Well, now you're his home health aide, as well." The doctor must have noticed the way her eyes were bulging out of her head, because she added, "You're surprised."

"That's one word for it," Nikki said with her mouth full.

"But Ken seemed very sure that you—"

"Have my friend here right over the proverbial barrel." Nikki started to laugh. "And to think," she added with typical irrepressibility, "I almost stayed home to watch the *Seinfeld* marathon!"

CHAPTER ◆ EIGHT

"So how's your stud-in-a-bed?" Nikki asked. She was standing with odd respectfulness outside Cathy's screen door.

"He's sleeping," she replied shortly. "What are you doing out there? Come in."

"Well, you *did* kill the last guest who took you by surprise," Nikki said, opening the screen door and stepping inside. "I'm the cautious type."

"My ass," Cathy said rudely.

"Oooh, more profanity! A new and, may I say, dark side of you. So, how's Shirtless?"

"Asleep. Don't you have a job?"

"And miss all this? No chance, killer."

"Do *not* start calling me that."

"Okay, okay, don't get mad, Psycho."

"Oh, God . . . Nikki . . ."

Her friend—ha!—took pity on her and set a bag
bulging with bakery goods on the table. "Brought breakfast! And seriously, Cath, I thought you might need a
hand the first day or so. So, I told work that my grandma
died—"

"Again? Nikki, they're bound to do the math one of
these days—"

"Minor details. So here I am, with three days off at
your disposal. Paid!"

"God help me. I mean, thank you." Cathy pulled the
bag toward her and opened it. Ah. Cream puffs, éclairs,
smiley-face sugar cookies. Bakeries were divine. The one
down the street, Rosie's, in particular. "I guess this works
out nicely. I had some vacation time I needed to burn or
I'd lose it, so I've got the rest of the week off, too."

"To play nursemaid?" Nikki asked, reaching for an
éclair and decimating it in two bites.

"I . . . guess so."

"Mm innfff afff oo, y'mmmmf."

"I know, but what could I do? Abandon him at the
hospital? He almost *died,* Nik. He did die, actually, for a
few minutes."

"Zzz mmm nnnt."

"I know, I know, but I think the punishment was quite
a bit worse than the crime, don't you? And I'm *not* being
taken advantage of," she added sharply as Nikki opened
her mouth to drool custard and make another point. "He
might have put my name on the forms, but it was still my
choice to have the ambulance drop him off here. In fact,
don't you think that's sad? That out of all the people in

the world, he listed a neighbor? Not even an old neighbor. A new one. I just—I just hope everybody's okay with it."

Jack hadn't made a sound since the accident. No helpful plates of cookies, no materializing car keys, no knocks. Nothing. Zip. It was funny how something initially scary had gotten comforting. His silence was making her distinctly nervous.

"Well, shoot, Cathy, I didn't think my opinion mattered so much," Nikki joked. "Hey, the only one who has to be okay with this is you. Me, I think you're nuts. But I've thought that since the seventh grade."

"Continuity," she mused. "How comforting."

"Amen," Nikki said, and selected a cream puff. "So, is he asleep or what?"

"I don't know," she confessed. "He was sleeping when the ambulance dropped him off. I've . . . I haven't gotten around to checking on him yet. The doctor said he needed lots of rest."

"Is he burned?"

"Not too badly. The shock was pretty quick. He's got some second-degree burns on the tips of his fingers and his feet and that's about it."

"He's likely to be a sucky patient. You know how men are. Okay, *you* don't, but take my word for it, they're total babies when they need to be taken care of."

"That's a cliché."

"For a reason, honeybun. Trust me, this guy's gonna be a pill."

"I suppose," she sighed.

"Well." Nikki popped the top off her cream puff, like taking the cap off a mushroom, and carefully licked out the whipped cream. "Go check. Get it over with."

Cathy drummed her fingers on the table and glanced at the stairs. "I suppose. The alternative is watching you eat."

"Hey, I got a bag full of cream puffs, honey. I could do this all morning."

Cathy got up to check on her new patient.

CHAPTER ◆ NINE

She rapped softly on the guest room door, heard nothing, and carefully eased the door open. Shirtless Ken was sitting up in bed, smiling at her. The fact that it was a genuine smile and not a leer was startling in itself, but there was something different about him. Not just the smile. Some fundamental change in his appearance, something she couldn't quite put her finger—

"Nice shirt," Nikki observed from behind her.

Ah-ha!

"Good morning, Nikki." Ken's smile widened, showcasing laugh lines around his gorgeous dark eyes. "Good morning, Cathy. I'm sorry to be so much trouble." His voice was deep and soft, and gone was Shirtless—er, Ken's—usual sneery whine.

"No problem," Nikki said, staring.

"I'm just so sorry you got hurt," Cathy added. Ken

was wearing a scrub top, doubtless loaned to him from someone at the hospital. His dark hair was mussed, and stubble bloomed along his jawline. "I feel . . . I feel . . . I feel . . ."

"Terrible," Nikki supplied helpfully.

"That is simply ridiculous, ladies," he said. "I can assure you the accident was entirely my fault. Why, I'm fortunate you're allowing me to stay here at all!"

Nikki stared at her watch. "How long has he been asleep?" she muttered. "What year is this?"

A fine question. Cathy was having a terrible time not staring. Not drooling, to be perfectly blunt. If Shirtless Ken had been ridiculously good-looking, Polite Ken was mesmerizing. Those dark eyes . . . almost knowing in their intensity, their—

"Really," he was saying, "I can't thank you enough."

"D'you want me to run over to your place, pick up some clothes or something?" Nikki offered.

"I couldn't put you to more trouble, Nikki."

Cathy cleared her throat. "Can I—would you—are you hungry?"

"Starving," he said softly, looking her straight in the eyes.

"One, two, three, swoon," Nikki said under her breath.

"I'll . . . I'll bring you some soup."

"Perhaps I should get it," Ken suggested. "I feel I'm imposing on you enough as it is."

"Don't be a dumbass," Nikki said. "You're supposed

to rest. We'll be back in a second. Don't so much as twitch out of that bed."

For a second, before she shut the door, Cathy thought she saw Ken blush. But that was ridiculous. The man threw epithets around like he was being paid for them.

"Oh my God," Nikki was rhapsodizing on the back stairs. She clutched her chest and wheezed like an asthmatic on the first day of spring. "Talk about turning over a new leaf! You should kill people more often!"

"Maybe he feels bad. What kind of soup do you think he'd like?"

"Maybe you have a helpless hunk in your bed and should stop babbling about soup. Those eyes! That hair! Ooh, the sexy unshaven look! God, he looks like an escapee from Studs and the Women Who Make Soup For Them."

"Tomato?"

"Cathy, I swear to God . . ." Nikki slumped into the closest kitchen chair. "Did you see the way he looked at you? All earnest and yummy?"

"Earnest and yummy?" she repeated, laughing in spite of herself. "Actually, I'm relieved. I thought he was going to be . . . ugly. Very ugly." In fact, she had been dreading the confrontation. "It makes logical sense; he was unpleasant *before* I accidentally killed him."

"Ken couldn't be ugly if you drew a mustache on him in black marker. Hell, red marker. I'm gonna go up and see if he needs a sponge bath."

"Nikki . . ."

"I was only going to do his testicles," she whined.

"Nikki, make yourself useful." Cathy tossed her friend a sponge. "And it's not what you're thinking. The dish soap is under the sink."

"Sure, while you tempt him with soup, you whore!"

"That's the plan," she replied smugly.

CHAPTER ◆ TEN

"Really, Cathy, I can feed myself," Ken teased. He gently took the spoon from her and she nearly tipped the bowl over at the shock of his warm fingers on hers. "I feel terrible to be putting you to so much trouble. The least I can do is dribble soup down my own chin."

"It's . . . it's no trouble."

"Well, I know you must have a job to worry about."

"I took some time off."

"Now I feel even guiltier," he said softly, but he smiled at her and she nearly drooped into a puddle beside the bed.

"They'll . . . they'll just have to get along without me at the office for a couple of days."

"This is very good, by the way."

"It's just . . . it's just from a can."

"Home made chicken soup is overrated," he said, and

laughed. Laughed! A deep, booming laugh that made her smile. She'd never heard him really laugh before. Sneer and chuckle nastily, yes. But a true laugh? "I used to hate my mother's chicken soup. She'd take a perfectly good chicken and wreck it with vegetables and overcooked noodles."

Cathy pounced. "Should I call her? Do you have *anybody* you'd like me to call?"

Ken's smile faltered. "No. No, there's no one. I'm the last of my family line."

"Oh. I am, too. Except for my father and his wife. I'm . . . I'm sorry."

"It's not your fault, Cathy. You've got to stop apologizing for events you can't control."

"Okay." She took the plunge. "But, um, but the fact that you're here flat on your, um, back for the week is very much my fault, and I—"

"Now, Cathy, we've been over this. I was stupid, and I paid the price. I'm grateful for the use of your guest room, and promise I won't be a burden on you much longer."

"You're not a burden," she said truthfully. She couldn't believe she was thinking it, much less saying it, but she added, "It's nice to have company. I'm still not used to living in such a big house by myself."

"You weren't really by yourself, though." He scraped the last of the noodles from the bottom of the bowl, then handed it to her.

"What?"

"Old houses have stories," he clarified. "Histories. It's hard to feel alone when you're in the middle of history."

"Oh. Hmm. Uh-huh. Ken, are you on any medication that I, as your hostess, should be made aware of?"

"Gosh," he said, handsome brow knitting in thought. "Not that I know of. Maybe some, what do you call them, antibiotics? You can check the bag the hospital sent me home with, if you like."

"Because you don't seem yourself. At all." Thank goodness! Still. Very odd. She'd been bracing herself for Sullen Shirtless Lawsuit Ken. This smiling, pleasant stranger in Ken's body was a complete shock. Argh. She shouldn't say shock.

"I know I seem different, Cathy," he was saying. "But there's a reason for it."

"There is?"

"Yes, of course. You've given me a second chance at life. I don't plan to waste it this time."

"Nikki helped."

There was something warm on her leg. She assumed he was experiencing a moment of incontinence, then realized he had rested his hand on her knee. "You're lucky to have a friend like Nikki," he was saying, "but she's not really my kind of girl."

"Oh yes? You mean the tall, gorgeous, fearless type? A real turn-off, huh?"

"I like them smart and petite, with cheekbones you could cut yourself on."

Totally weirded out, she moved her now-sweaty knee

away from New and Improved Ken. "Oh. Well. That's, um, nice. Would you like more soup?"

"I think I'll rest now, if you don't mind."

"Okay." She stood. "Just, um, yell or something if you need anything."

"Of course. Thank you again for the fine lunch, Cathy. But it's Cathleen, isn't it?"

"What?"

"That's what it is, for real."

"Nobody . . . I mean, everyone calls me Cathy."

"Yes, but Cathleen suits you better."

"Okay. Have a nice nap."

Completely mystified, she walked out, feeling his gaze on her until she closed the door.

CHAPTER ELEVEN

"Okay," Nikki was saying as Cathy not-so-ceremoniously shoved her toward the door, "*I* have an annoying neighbor, too, and while he isn't quite as yummilicious as Ken, he's definitely got potential, so if you could just come over and kill him—" She teetered on the steps, and Cathy gave her one more gentle shove. Arms pinwheeling, Nikki went down. "Aigh! All right, all right. At least think it over, willya?"

"Good night, Nikki." She shut the screen door, then locked it for good measure. Friends, she added to herself. The ultimate mixed blessing.

And speaking of friends, she'd been missing one lately.

"Jack?" she whispered in the kitchen. "Are you there? It's okay if you've been hiding because of all the ruckus lately, but it should settle down soon."

Nothing.

"And me without my car keys," she joked, which was a lie, as she knew right where they were. Still, Jack had been unable to resist finding them before.

Nothing. Dead silence.

She gave up and climbed the stairs to bed.

Cathy woke hours later, scared out of her wits and not understanding why.

Then she realized why: her bed was shaking. Not trembling, not twitching, *shaking*. It was sliding forward, then would slam back against the wall hard enough to nearly throw her to the floor. Then the performance would repeat. And repeat.

"Jack!" she screamed, clutching wildly at the bedsheets. "Jack! Stop it! Jaaaaaaaaaaaaaack!"

The door to her room was thrown open and there was Ken, walking calmly toward the madness. "I apologize for not knocking," he said as he bent and scooped her up.

"You shouldn't . . . you shouldn't be up. You have to rest; the doctor said you have to rest. Don't let go of me," she begged.

"Never. Besides, I can't sleep in this noise," he pointed out, kicking her bedroom door shut behind them. She could still hear the thumping of her bed, but it was growing fainter . . . either because Jack was getting tired, or because Ken was taking her so rapidly, efficiently away from the noise.

"There, now," he said, tucking her into the left side of his bed.

"He's never . . . he's never been like that before," she said, almost gulped. Why were silly things like bouncing beds so terrifying when it was dark out? She'd probably be laughing about it in the morning. "I know you'll think it sounds silly, but he's—"

"Houses have history, remember?" he asked, climbing into bed beside her.

"Um . . . Ken . . ."

"Don't worry," he said, kissing the tips of her fingers, then releasing her and rolling over on his back. "I know you're not that kind of girl."

I'm not?

"Thanks for coming to get me," she said softly in the dark.

"I'll always come to get you," he replied, and she supposed that should sound creepy, like something out of the Stalker's Handbook, but instead it was so darned comforting she fell right back to sleep.

CHAPTER ◆ TWELVE

Ken was gone when she woke up, thank God, because Nikki was standing over her, leering. Needless to say, a startling way to begin the day.

"Don't start," she said shortly, throwing back the quilts and standing. Atypically hot spring or not, her toes instantly froze to the floorboards. Socks, her kingdom for wool socks! "I mean it, Nik."

"Oh, I don't think so, Slutty McGee. Normally your cool exterior would be off-putting, but not today! Here I am, coming over early to help you with your own personal Ken doll, and I find you in his bed!"

"It wasn't like that, Nikki. He—"

"That's the worst part! I know it wasn't like that; I can't *believe* it. You can't even be loose right. Dope. Otherwise you two would be having a little morning fun, uh-huh, uh-huh . . ." Nikki wiggled her butt for emphasis—like any was needed—in concert with her eyebrows. "And instead, you're in here snoring like a beagle and he's in the kitchen doing the dishes."

"He's doing the *what?*" Then, "I don't snore."

Nikki held up a hand. "Scout's honor, baby. How many slumber parties have we been to? You snore like a beast. None of us can figure out how such a tiny person makes such a big scary noise."

"Cathleen! Nikki!"

"That's him," she said, looking toward the open doorway. She hurried across the hall to her room and grabbed a pair of sweatpants and a T-shirt. "That's Ken, calling us."

"Well, duh," Nikki said, and slurped her coffee from the mug she was holding. "Thanks for the exposition. Oh, and is that what you're wearing to seduce wayward boy-toys these days? The holes over the left knee are an especially attractive touch. Was it barf green when you bought it, or did it just get that way over repeated washings?"

"Breakfast!"

"I hate you." Nikki sighed, following Cathy out the door.

"Well, I hate you, too," she pointed out reasonably. "Besides, I told you, it's not like that."

"Uh-huh. Still hating you—whoa!" Nikki ducked, and just in time, because the portrait she'd passed by in the hall suddenly hurled itself to the floor, missing her by inches. "You need bigger nails, girlfriend," she said, picking up the picture and leaning it carefully against the wall. "Ugh, what is it with the poor slobs in these old-fashioned portraits? Why do they all look embalmed?"

"They didn't have instant flash back then," Cathy explained. She stood on tiptoes to see over Nikki's shoulder. "They would have to hold a pose for twenty minutes. That's why you never see anyone smiling in old pictures."

"More important, why is it still hanging here in your hallway?"

"The last owner left quite a few of her things behind. I told her I'd work on getting them packed away, nicely and neatly. It's part of the reason I got such a good deal."

"Those are the Carrolls," Ken said from behind them, making both women jump. He pointed his spatula at the stiff-looking family. "They built this house. That was the father, Jerome, and that was his wife, Janice. They had two children: Victoria, and Jefferson."

"That's enthralling," Nikki said. "Really, and I mean that. I'll take my eggs over easy."

He smiled at her which, stupidly, made Cathy feel jealous as hell. "Yes, Nikki, and good morning. I also have some nice fried ham, and chocolate milk."

"Baby, that's a date!" she cried, sashaying past him into the kitchen.

"How did you know about the family who used to live here?"

"My neighbor," he said easily. "Victoria is the one who sold the house to you."

"I—I never met her. I just met with her lawyer." She distinctly remembered Ken referring to Victoria as "that fucking old bitch." Cripes. He really *did* turn over a new leaf. Maybe Nikki had a point. Maybe she should electrocute men more often.

You need more sleep, she told herself. When Nikki starts to make sense, it's time to go to the doctor for some nice pills.

He came closer—luckily it was a *gigantic* hallway—and brushed one of her dark curls out of her eyes. "Did you sleep well? After the . . . unpleasantness?"

"Like the dead. I mean, like a log. I mean, thanks for coming. Coming to get me, I mean. I would have been scared to be here by myself."

"There's nothing to be scared of as long as I'm here." Then he colored, which was odd to see on such a large man. "Not that I'm planning to overstay my welcome. I just . . . just wanted to set your mind at ease, is what I meant to say."

"Well, I'm sorry if I scared you. Screaming like that. Like an idiot."

"As a matter of fact, you *did* scare me. I was relieved to find you weren't being murdered."

"No, just haunted."

"Yes, about that. I think—"

"I don't want to talk about that right now," she said nervously.

"Well, I'm ready to talk when you are. Like I said, I just want to set your mind at ease."

"And *I*," Nikki said, poking her head around the corner, "want you to set my stomach at ease. Come on, you two can make goo-goo eyes at each other later. Cook, boy, cook!"

"Sorry," Cathy muttered, but was gratified to see Ken hide a smile.

CHAPTER ◆ THIRTEEN

"Girlfriend, you are eggless."

Caught dreamily contemplating Ken's shoulders, Cathy blinked. "What?"

"Eggless. Egg free. You're out. You got no more. And you're low on milk. *And* you're ugly."

"She certainly is not," Ken said, offended.

"Tell me," Nikki sighed. "Try going to a club with her sometime. I loooooove being 'the funny one.'"

"Shut up," Cathy said, blushing. "Well, I suppose—"

"I'll go to the store," Ken quickly offered. "That is, if Nikki will let me use her car. Mine's . . . um . . ."

"I thought you lost your license," Cathy said. "Too many DUIs."

"Oh. Well, no. But I don't have a car of my own. Anymore."

"Shoot, you can borrow mine. I'll come with you!"

"She doesn't like to drive," Cathy explained.

"It's not that I don't like it," Nikki said, pushing back her chair, "it's that it's the most mind-numbing chore on the planet. I'd rather garden. Or shave a goat. Seriously."

"Let me get my wallet," Cathy said.

"No, I should—"

"Ken, let her pay, she can afford it. Stingy cow has the first nickel she ever made."

"I do not! But Nikki's right," Cathy said, practically forcing the dreadful phrase past her teeth. "I'm supposed to be taking care of you."

"So you don't sue her for this lovely house!"

"And the least I can do is pay for groceries," she added, glaring at her friend.

Ken laughed. "I'm not going to sue you."

"Sure, say that now," Nikki replied. "Cath, I think you've got more potatoes in the cellar." A hank of blond hair escaped from her cap, and Nikki absently tucked it back up. "You're just low on dairy stuff."

"Would you mind running down to the basement and getting them, Ken? I—"

"I need to change my shirt," he said abruptly. "Nikki can do it."

Nikki's eyebrows arched, and Cathy knew how she felt. Since the accident, Ken had been so polite and soft-spoken, it was odd to hear him actually refuse to do a favor.

Nikki shrugged. "Your shirt is fine. Let's go, handsome. Shotgun."

"What?"

"Never mind. Back in a few, Cathy. Make yourself useful while we're gone and, I dunno, do the dishes or something."

"Oh, hush up," she muttered.

Two hours later

She was wiping down the counters, vainly hoping Jack would make his presence known, when she heard the unmistakable sound of a car stalling, starting, stalling, and jerking its way up the driveway. She stepped out onto her front porch in time to see Nikki roll out from her door like a paratrooper in a World War II movie.

"What the hell?" Cathy began.

"The ground, I kiss the sweet sweet ground of life!" Nikki yowled, and then proceeded to do just that, smacking the turf with her lips. Cathy heard the car's engine stall, and then Ken got out and stood awkwardly beside the car, anxiously watching Nikki roll around the yard like she'd been knifed in the dairy section. "My life flashed before my eyes! Six times! And let me tell you, I need to date more!"

"I guess I'm a little out of practice," Ken explained, reddening.

"A little! You're a wheel psychotic with absurdly well-built delts! You're a—"

"Nikki, calm down." Cathy helped her friend off the grass. "For heaven's sake. You're not exactly an expert behind the wheel, either, all the chauffeuring we all have to do for you. Serves you right."

"I nearly *die* and it serves me right? You suck!"

"Are you"—Cathy put up a palm to cover her twitching lips—"all right?"

"Just a little humiliated," Ken confessed.

"You should be a little *concussed,* the way you cut off that school bus!"

"Nikki, you're getting hysterical."

"Damn right I am!"

"I am sorry," Ken said again. "I won't drive you again until I'm better at it."

"Now with the threats," Cathy teased. "Who do you think will get stuck with the duty?"

Ken slipped an arm around her waist and, surprised, she let him. His tentative hug was nothing like his earlier, beery gropings. "Next time you should come with us," he said. "Keep me out of trouble."

"Oh, barf," Nikki said, and stomped into the house.

"You forgot the groceries!" Cathy called after her, and got the one-fingered salute in return.

CHAPTER ◆ FOURTEEN

"So are you going to jump his bones or what?"

"Aaiigh!" Cathy nearly fell out of the easy chair. "Nikki! I thought you went home!"

"Yeah, well, I forgot my magazines. So I'm back. So? Are you?"

"Keep your voice down."

"So, no."

"None of your business." Cathy lowered her voice to a whisper. "Besides, he's recovering from dying."

"That's always your excuse for not getting laid." Nikki said this in a perfectly normal tone of voice.

Cathy burst out laughing. "Be quiet! He'll hear you."

"Oh, yeah? Where is he? Scrubbing your grout? Cleaning out your fridge?"

"He went to bed. He's tired and his burns were bothering him."

"What burns?"

"They're faint," Cathy said defensively, "but painful."

"Yeah, yeah, whatever. So why don't you go up there with some, I dunno, salve or whatever. Minister to him, like."

"You've been downloading too much porn again."

"I live alone; what *else* am I going to do? And what are you waiting for, dumbass? Seduce!"

"He's a little shy."

Nikki snorted.

"Now, I mean," she amended. "In fact, he's practically like another person."

"Yeah, so, he saw the light at the end of the tunnel and jumped off the track before it could run him over, or whatever. Good for him. Seduce!"

"I'm not you, Nikki." She did not say this defensively; she was what she was. "I can't just go up there and strip and stand on his bed like Venus on the half shell."

"When was the last time I did *that?*" Nikki had finally gathered up the last of her magazines and was impatiently jingling her keys. "Look, Cath, it's not just that he's gorgeous. Although he could definitely give Tom Cruise a run for his money. Plus, unlike certain ex-spouses of Nicole Kidman, Ken's not short."

"We're getting off the subject."

"We never left it, baby! It's just that you don't seem . . . I mean, you're kind of lonesome. You've got your house and your temp jobs and your weekly duty phone call and once in a while I manage to drag you out of here and go to a club and that's all." Nikki faltered; she preferred to hide her emotions behind wisecracks. "And I-I just think you could use something else, is all. And he seems like he really likes you."

"Seems like he really likes me? You should write get-well cards."

"Blow me, how's that for a card?"

"Nikki, don't you think you're being just a bit inconsistent? After all, you were pushing him at me when he was a tiresome blowhard."

"Cathy, that's totally the definition of consistent. Besides, now he's *not*. So what's the problem?"

"That it's gauche to take advantage of someone relying on my hospitality?"

"Picky, picky. Besides . . . whoops!" Nikki dodged just as another family portrait fell off the wall and slammed to the floor hard enough to crack the glass in the frame. "Cripes, how many of these things do you have around here?"

"Lots," she admitted. "Mind the glass. And I'll think about what you said, Nikki."

"Liar," she said, not unkindly, and started to leave, carefully sidestepping the broken glass. "I'd help you clean up, but you know, that's just not me."

"I know she's a pain," Cathy said after she heard Nikki's car vroom off. "But stop throwing pictures at her, Jack. I mean it, now. You've been sulking for ages and now you're acting in a distinctively unpleasant manner. Don't make me call an exorcist!" How, she thought, does one call an exorcist, anyway? The Yellow Pages? Word-of-mouth referral? "Stop it *this* minute."

Or what, she thought, but nothing else happened, so she was spared having to think about it. Instead, she finished *Chicken Soup for the Haunted Soul,* and went to bed.

CHAPTER ◆ FIFTEEN

Cathy lay awake for a long time. It was late. Past 2:00 A.M. Waking had been a little like dreaming, or swimming: inch by inch through consciousness until she was completely awake, with no idea how she had gotten there, or why.

Then she heard it. Low, guttural moaning. So low and quiet it took her a minute to realize she was hearing anything.

Ken. It was coming from Ken's room.

She got out of bed at once, her feet freezing on the wooden floor, and hurried out her bedroom door and down the hall. A picture swung ominously as she passed it, but didn't fall.

Ken's door was open and she stepped inside without hesitation.

"Ken? What's wrong?"

No answer. He had torn the sheets free of the bed and they were balled up around his middle, and his fists were working restlessly through the cotton. Moonlight fell across the bed and she could see the sweat sheening his body.

She stepped to his bed and shook his shoulder, which was as rigid as stone.

"Don't go in the basement," he said very clearly, and his eyes popped open. Cathy nearly screamed, and in shock her hand clamped down on his shoulder, probably hurting him. His eyes. It had been like looking into the eyes of a dead man.

"K-Ken? Are you all right? I heard . . . heard . . ."

"Cathy, thank God," he muttered, and pulled on her hand, pulled her to him until she was beside him in the bed.

"Are you all right?" she whispered as he stroked her face.

"I am now," he replied. "Stay with me."

"*You're* sort of staying with *me*," she teased to cover her nervousness. She heard an odd sound, then placed it: pictures swinging against the wall in the hallway, but not falling. Jack must not be up for a full-blown temper tantrum tonight. "But sure. I'll stay."

He leaned in and kissed her so softly, it was almost tentative. She was a little surprised—she hadn't expected Ken to be tentative between the sheets, ever—but pleased. She had never been one for a big choking tongue being rammed down her throat. Little butterfly kisses were more her style.

She sat up and pulled her nightgown over her head. "Don't start," she told him before he could. "I'm well aware I look like an extra in *Little House on the Prairie* in this thing."

"I like it," he said seriously. Then he laughed. "It beats what I wore to bed today."

"Yes," she murmured, tracing her fingers across his shoulders, circling his nipples. "We've simply got to go over to your place tomorrow and get you more clothes."

"Tomorrow," he said.

"Yes. Tomorrow."

"Butterfly kisses," she said dreamily, half an hour later.

"Pardon?" She was cuddled against him, spoon-style, and he was kissing the back of her neck and shoulder.

And that wasn't all he had kissed. Even now, she could still feel his mouth on her—well, his mouth *was* on her—and shivered. He had been all hands and mouth and tongue, all hungry skill and silent desire. When he had finally entered her, he had done so because she had been begging him to. When he was inside her, she had locked her ankles behind his back and never, never wanted him to go.

They had rocked together for an eternity, one that was over much too soon. Not that she wasn't ready to be done—she had stopped counting climaxes after six— but beyond the physical pleasure, the *connection* they had shared was so intense, she didn't want it to end.

It had never been like that. She had never *dreamed* it could be like that.

Now they were sweating lightly in the cool dark, and she could feel beard burn where he had kissed and licked and sucked her nipples. She welcomed the mild discomfort. It proved what had happened was real.

"You're so beautiful," he said. "I've always thought so." He reached out and tugged at one of her curls, watching as it bounced back. "But not very many people know how clever and funny you are. It's like a wonderful secret."

"I don't know that it's a *wonderful* secret," she began.

"But you're so quick to denigrate yourself. Why is that?"

"I-I don't know. Nikki's the pretty one, the funny one. I'm just . . . me, Cathy."

"Nikki has her charms," he agreed, "but she's not you."

"Definitely not," she agreed. "Never mind. How come you weren't so nice before I killed you? We could have gotten together a lot sooner."

He didn't say anything, and she cursed herself. "I'm sorry," she said quickly. "That was in poor taste."

"No, that's fine," he replied, obviously meaning the opposite. "I-I have no excuse for how I acted earlier. I was . . . I didn't . . . things were different then."

"Well, all right." She could see how tense he had become; the forearm she was lying against had become hard as iron. "The important thing is, you're here now."

"Yes," he said. "I'm here now."

She leaned forward and kissed him, savoring his mouth, his sweet, firm mouth. He caressed her curls for a moment, then kissed the tip of her ear and cuddled her more firmly into his side.

As they both drifted back to sleep, Cathy had a passing thought that shocked her and left her rigid and wakeful for the next hour.

She had been, in her defense, a little distracted at the time. But while they had been rocking together, while his delicious cock had filled her up, had stroked sweetly, while her hands groped and held and groped some more, while his face had nuzzled into the crook of her neck, she had started calling his name.

And he had covered her mouth. Gently, but firmly. Covered her mouth so she couldn't say anything.

In an instant, she had it. And was furious it had taken her so long to catch on.

My God, she thought. I'm sharing a bed with a dead man.

When she knew he was deeply asleep, she slipped out of his bed.

CHAPTER ◆ SIXTEEN

"I just want to see Miss Carroll for a couple of minutes," Cathy explained. "I called earlier? Cathy Wyth?"

"Oh, yes . . . Wyth. Well, of course Miss Carroll is always happy to have visitors. It's down the hall on your left, Room 326."

Cathy thanked the nurse and hurried down the nursing home hallway. She had been afraid that tracking down the original owner of her house would be tricky, especially since Victoria Carroll did all her business through her lawyer. But it only took a few phone calls.

Miss Carroll was a surprise. For one thing, though she was sitting in a wheelchair by the window, she was perfectly erect, and her hands, slim and pretty, were busy with a pile of knitting.

For another, she was beautiful. Not "gee, I can see she was pretty when she was younger" beautiful.

Beautiful-right-now beautiful. Her long hair was un-
bound and flowed over her shoulders and back, and was
pure white. Her face, while heavily bracketed with
laugh lines, was porcelain pure, with a wide forehead
and a narrow, foxy chin. Her eyes were the green-brown
of a pond in the deep woods.

"Hello," she said, looking up from her knitting.
"How are you liking the house?"

"Oh, you . . . you know who I am?" Cathy was curs-
ing herself for making assumptions. Just because the
older woman chose to do all her business through a
lawyer didn't mean she was lacking, either mentally or
physically. "I mean, I—"

"The desk announced you. And your name was on all
the paperwork I received this week. Would you like a
pop? Some coffee?"

"No, I-I just wanted to . . . I was just interested in
your family."

"My family." Miss Carroll commenced knitting, her
bright purple needles flashing in the morning light. "My
family is all dead, Miss Wyth. All except for me."

"Yes, I . . . yes." Cathy sat on the edge of the bed,
suddenly feeling foolish. Where was she supposed to go
with this? Hi, thanks for selling me your house, I think
it's haunted? And what was Victoria Carroll supposed to
do about that, exactly?

"I'm ready to go," she continued. "I've been ready
for a long time. I never had any children, never even got
married. I miss my brother, and I miss my parents. I'm
ready to go home."

"Your brother?"

"Mmm. Jefferson. Oh, that was a terrible day."

"A terrible day?" Then, "Jefferson?"

"We were horsing around, you know, like kids do—although we didn't think we were kids *then,* certainly not—and my brother was home from Harvard. He was so happy to be home! He said nobody on the coast could cook like our mother, and we started chasing each other. It was so silly and childish. Then he tripped on the basement stairs." Miss Carroll dropped a stitch, then stopped knitting altogether. "There wasn't a mark on him, isn't that strange? Nobody could get over it. How handsome he was at his funeral, like he was sleeping. But his neck was broken and that was that. One minute we were laughing and tearing around, and the next we were planning a funeral."

Don't go in the basement.

"So Jefferson . . . your brother . . ."

"Oh, he's the ghost living in your house." Victoria Carroll was looking right at Cathy; no hiding behind knitting this time. "I was so upset. I blamed myself for his death for years and years. Couldn't leave the house, never got married. Never had a life outside of my family's, and once my parents passed on, there was . . . nothing. And I guess my brother stayed around. Looked after me. He always hoped I would move on. And I did, just a couple of weeks ago. But I think . . . I think the habit of staying in the house, it was too strong." She paused. "We always called him Jack, you know."

It was a good thing, Cathy decided, that she was sitting down. Because she felt as if she were falling. "No," she said faintly. "That's not how it works. You're supposed to have no idea what I'm talking about, and I'm supposed to help you sort of work around to it, and then it'll be this dramatic revelation, not a . . . not a matter-of-fact story where you just blurt out, oh, by the way, the ghost is my brother Jack. Didn't you know?"

"Sorry, darling, but I don't have that kind of time."

"I guess I'm the one who's sorry. I sort of assumed you . . . you wouldn't know what was going on. But you do know."

"I honestly thought he would either leave when I sold the house," Miss Carroll said, "or come with me. I wasn't tricking you. I have to admit, I kind of miss him. How is he?"

"He's taken over the body of my obnoxious next-door neighbor. And now my neighbor is the ghost." Cathy sighed. "I should have kept renting."

"Oh." She brightened. "So he's alive again?"

"Well . . . yeah."

Miss Carroll clapped. "Wonderful!"

"No. My neighbor . . . he's stuck in some sort of limbo, he's—"

"You're not talking about Ken, are you?" Miss Carroll's mouth thinned with distaste. "I wouldn't worry about *him,* dear. Anything that happened to him, he had it coming."

"Yes, but he's *in my house,*" Cathy said, exasperated. "Living with a ghost might be business as usual for you, Miss Carroll, but it's a pain in my ass!"

"Well, yes, if the ghost is Ken. Jacky was a *wonderful* ghost. So helpful."

Cathy flopped back onto the bed. "My head hurts."

"You're just Jack's type, too," Miss Carroll commented, picking up her knitting. "All that dark curly hair, those big eyes . . ."

"Don't start on my curly hair and big eyes, please. What should I do?"

"Marry my brother," she said promptly.

"About. The. Ghost."

"Oh, I'm old so I know about exorcisms? Call a priest, dear. Or don't. Ken struck me as the type who withers without attention. He'll probably go away on his own."

"You know, there's the small matter of your brother taking over a body that didn't belong to him."

"Bullshit," Miss Carroll said. "Jacky was cheated out of his own lifetime. Dead at twenty-one; you call that reasonable? What was Ken doing with the body, anyway? Riddling it with STDs? Filling it with alcohol and getting DUI's? Using it to date rape unsuspecting women? Why shouldn't my brother have a chance?"

Because it was wrong. Because the body didn't belong to him. Because it was creepy. Because she didn't mean to kill Ken. Because nothing was that simple. "I . . . I don't know."

"Exactly." Miss Carroll held up her knitting, then reached into the bag at her feet and withdrew a new ball of yarn. The yarn exactly matched her knitting needles. "Give my love to Jacky when you see him."

CHAPTER ◆ SEVENTEEN

Cathy slammed into her house and stomped into the kitchen. "You've got a lot of explaining to do, buster!"

"Yeah!" Nikki added, wiping up the last of the egg yolk on her plate with her toast. "What are we doing?"

"Nikki, go away. This is between me and Jack. And don't park in my spot anymore; I almost rear-ended you this morning."

"Uh-huh. His name is Ken, dear."

"Hush up. Go to the bakery. Go to the bathroom. Something."

"You figured it out." Ken-Jack looked absurdly relieved. And adorable, with the dish towel slung over one shoulder. He smelled like Dawn detergent. "I thought you might. I've been trying and trying to think of how to tell you—"

"My ass!"

"Ooooh," Nikki said.

"You've only had a million chances to bring it up and you blew it every time. How about after we made love last night, buster? Huh? How about then?"

"Jesus, I can't leave this place for one night without all hell breaking loose," Nikki commented.

Jack put his hands on her shoulders, dark eyes serious. "Cathy, you're right."

"I *know* I'm right. I'm not an idiot. Nikki?"

"That's right," she said. "She's not an idiot."

"I meant go away."

"I should have told you," Jack was saying. "But to be honest, I couldn't think how. I was afraid I'd scare you. There just isn't a nice way to say 'when Ken died I took over his body' without sounding like a bad man. And I would never want you to think I was a bad man. I love you, Cathy. I'd do anything for you."

"Oh. Well . . ." She chewed on her lower lip. "You're kind of taking the wind out of my sails, here . . ."

"Let me get this straight," Nikki began. "Your house was haunted by this guy, who, when you killed Ken off in a fit of rage—"

"I did *not*—"

"—took over Shirtless Ken's body. Well, who's knocking down all the pictures?"

"Ken," Cathy and Jack said in unison.

"Man, no wonder he's pissed. Not only did you steal his body and put the moves on his girl, he's now regulated to the spirit world and stuck in this termite trap? Bogus!"

"You're taking this awfully well," Cathy said suspiciously.

"I'm the one who keeps getting almost eye-gouged with flying glass," Nikki reminded her. "And Ken *was* an asshole. This whole passive-aggressive crap would be just like him. It makes sense, sort of."

"I want you to know," Jack said, his hands still warm on her shoulders, which was unbelievably distracting, "that I didn't take over Ken's body. I was sort of . . . sort of pulled into it. You'll never know and I don't have the words . . . I was so happy when I woke up in the hospital. I couldn't believe I'd been given a second chance after all these years. A second chance—"

"Ugh, don't say it," Nikki warned.

"—with you."

"Okay, I'm officially barfed out now."

"Shut *up,* Nikki. Really, Jack?"

"Why else do you think I wanted to come back here? Not just because I grew up here. I wanted to be close to you. When my sister moved away, I thought it would be my time to just . . . leave. But then I saw you . . . you looked so . . . so lost and so determined. And you were so pretty . . ."

"And don't forget about her cute split ends."

"Nikki!"

Jack laughed. "I even liked your friend."

"Did you like me, or did you *like* me like me?"

"Nikki."

"And I-I couldn't leave. When I heard you talking on the phone with your family, I thought, this woman is alive, and she's as lonely as I am. And I just . . . couldn't leave you."

"Thanks," Nikki commented. "Thanks a lot. What am I, chopped liver?"

"Nikki, get it through your head: this is not about you." She looked back up at Jack. "I went to see your sister today, Jack. She told me everything. About what happened to you in the basement. About why you never left her."

"I'd like to go see her, too. If I could just get you to drive me—"

"That's" why you're a shittier driver than me," Nikki said. "You're about a hundred years out of practice!"

"Not quite a hundred," Jack said dryly. "It's—"

"Basement!"

Jack flinched. "Don't do that."

"Okay. Basement!"

"I'd kill her, except I get the feeling she'd never leave," Cathy said, glaring at her friend.

"What are we going to do about Ken?" Nikki asked. "We can't just let him hang around knocking pictures off the walls."

"What is this 'we' stuff?" Cathy asked. "And frankly, I have no idea."

"It's very difficult to manifest," Jack said quietly. "If I affected something in the physical world, it would often take days to build my strength back up. And I had things to hang on for. My sister, for example. Ken . . . Ken has nothing but his anger."

"Well, he was a pretty angry guy . . ."

Jack shook his head. "It's not enough. It's really not." He squeezed Cathy's fingers. "Love is. Love can last for years. Anger . . . anger wears off."

"Barf again. So he'll just . . . just fade away?"

"Something like that."

Relieved, Cathy said, "As long as he can't hurt anyone on the way out."

"You could take a vacation," Nikki suggested. "You've already got the time off from work. Go to an island or Disney World or something. Maybe . . . get to know each other. I bet when you come back, Ken will be long gone."

Jack smiled. "What a wonderful idea."

"I agree," Cathy said. "Plus, if we're not here, we won't have pop-in guests every third hour."

"What, I'm not going with you guys?"

"Forget it, Nik."

"Nikki, you're very nice," Jack began tactfully, "but—"

"No you're not," Cathy said. Impulsively she squeezed Jack so hard his eyes bulged. "Besides, this is me-and-Jack time. No pals allowed."

"So that's it? You're gonna take off with a guy who's been haunting your house for a zillion years? A guy you barely know? That's not like you, Cath."

"I know," she said, and smiled at Jack.

Turn the page for a special preview of
Janelle Denison's next novel

BORN TO BE WILDE

Coming soon from Berkley Sensation!

"I need your help."

Startled by the desperate request drifting through the phone line, Joel Wilde's fingers tightened around the cordless receiver pressed to his ear. It had been years since he'd heard that voice, but he recognized it instantly. A friend. A comrade. The man who'd literally saved his life.

"Zach?" he asked incredulously.

"Yeah, buddy, it's me." Zach Marshall's forced chuckle fell flat. "It's been a while, huh?"

Over four years, to be exact, Joel thought as he sat down on one of the bar stools in his kitchen. As Marine's they'd been assigned to the same unit, and after serving their country for six years, they'd both opted not to re-enlist. Their last mission in Somalia had been harrowing, to the point that neither of them had been eager to repeat such an unpleasant experience. Joel wanted to join the real world again and live a normal life, free from strict rules, relentless, rigorous missions, and being responsible for other men's lives.

After being honorably discharged, he and Zach had spent two weeks together living it up—carousing and partying with a bevy of willing women, and making up for all the wild, frivolous fun they'd missed out on during their tour of duty. Then they'd gone their separate ways—with Zach driving off to Atlantic City with his wallet filled with the savings he'd accumulated during his time in the Marines, and Joel heading back to Chicago where he'd grown up, to figure out what he was going to do with his life now that he was no longer a part of the U.S. Marine Corp.

He'd spent nearly two years doing oddball jobs before going into business with three fellow ex-Marines as security agents. They'd formed ESS Group, Elite Security Specialists, and were hired to do everything from setting up security at venues and special events, protecting high-profile clients, and undercover work when it was warranted. In just a few years time, the company had become one of Chicago's top respected security firms.

He'd tried to keep in touch with Zach over the years, but Zach was a wanderer, always seeking action and adventure. He was a good guy at heart, but unfortunately, because of the chronic problem he had with drinking and gambling, he usually found trouble instead. Which brought Joel back to the reason behind his friend's call.

"What's going on, Zach?" Joel was compelled to ask, but dreaded the answer.

"I'm in trouble. *Big* trouble." Zach's voice cracked with the faintest hint of despair. "I owe a bookie a shit load of money that I don't have."

Joel wasn't surprised, just disappointed that his friend hadn't changed his ways. Obviously Zach hadn't learned his lesson after one of their comrades, Bruno, had beat the crap out of Zach when he'd neglected to pay up the five hundred bucks he'd lost to the big, burly Marine during a poker game while they'd been serving in Somalia.

Joel blew out a rough stream of breath. "How much?"

A noticeable pause ensued before Zach finally answered. "Over fifty grand."

Joel's mind reeled with disbelief, and a ripe curse escaped his lips before he could stop it. "Jesus, Zach, I don't have that kind of cash to give you."

"I know, and I swear I'm not asking you for it," Zach tried to assure him. "But this situation involves more than just me. Remember my sister, Lora?"

They'd never met personally, but Joel did, indeed, remember bits and pieces about Lora Marshall. Zach had openly shared the amusing letters his sister had written to him on a weekly basis during their stint in the Marines, and the occasional picture she'd sometimes include along with the correspondence.

It had been a very long time since Joel had seen any of those photos, or even thought of Lora Marshall, but as he closed his eyes her features easily filled his mind.

She'd possessed a lovely face with soft, pretty features, which was framed by her rich, shoulder-length brown hair that looked shiny and silky to the touch. He recalled being drawn to her laughing, inviting blue eyes, and a smile that was both sweet and sensual in an understated way.

Joel's gut clenched at the thought of Zach putting her life in jeopardy somehow. "What does your sister have to do with any of this?"

"I need you to watch over her and make sure she's protected," Zach said on a quick rush of breath. "These people I'm dealing with want their money badly . . . and there's a good chance they'll be looking for her."

Joel jammed his fingers through his too long hair and frowned, not liking the direction this conversation was taking. "And why would they be looking for Lora?"

The silence that followed was deafening.

"Dammit, Zach," he bit out harshly, his own anger rising swiftly to the surface. "You can't just drop something like this on me and not tell me what the hell is going on. If your sister's life is at risk, in any way at all, I need details, *all of them,* in order to keep her safe."

"Okay, I'll tell you everything you need to know." Zach's tone was more subdued now, to match the grave situation. "Just promise me that no matter what, you'll look after her until I get this mess taken care of. I might have to disappear for a while, and she doesn't have anyone else. I need to know that she's in good hands, and you're the only one I trust to keep her safe from any harm."

Joel absently rubbed a hand over his jean clad thigh, right where a puckered scar resided—an ugly, glaring reminder of how Zach had once risked his own life to save his during a covert mission. Joel *owed* him, and while Zach hadn't come right out and said as much, Joel was certain that his friend was counting on that return favor now.

Keeping an eye on Zach's sister was the least Joel could do for his friend. "You have my word," he promised.

BERKLEY SENSATION
COMING IN DECEMBER 2005

Dead Reckoning
by Linda Castillo
Linda Castillo is "at the top of her game" (*All About Romance*) with this romantic thriller about a D.A. with a dark secret and a shadowy past.

0-425-20720-X

Taste of Temptation
by Amelia Grey
Chaos ensues when a notorious rake and a darling of the ton are sent unwillingly to the altar.

0-425-20721-8

The Lady Killer
by Samantha Saxon
The smash follow-up to *The Lady Lies* set in the tumultuous era of the Napoleonic Wars.

0-425-20732-3

Strange Attractions
by Emma Holly
A hot novel of one woman's sensual education in the hands of a reclusive professor.

0-425-20503-7